ChangelingPress.com

Dragon Stones
Paranormal Women's Fiction
Stephanie Burke

Dragon Stones
Paranormal Women's Fiction
Stephanie Burke

ISBN: 978-1-60521-873-1

Publisher:
Changeling Press LLC
315 N. Centre St.
Martinsburg, WV 25404
ChangelingPress.com

Printed in the U.S.A.

Editor: Treva Harte
Cover Artist: Bryan Keller

The individual stories in this anthology have been previously released in E-Book format.

Table of Contents

Dragon Stone (Dragon 1)
A Paranormal Women's Fiction Novella
Stephanie Burke

In the human world, Prince Vulwin Valas is known as Win Arcarius, openly gay, very promiscuous, and one of the most highly sought after models ever. To the Fae Realms, he is known as the Silver Shadow, the King's assassin, and someone not to be crossed.

A routine visit home suddenly becomes more complicated, and Vulwin finds himself with a new mate, a new enemy, and a future he never considered before with... a dragon.

Iffear comes to Vulwin at his most vulnerable, but as magical enemies and a plot to destroy the Dhrovish throne make themselves known, the newly mated couple finds themselves drawing closer together in order to survive.

Chapter One

Vulwin would have never noticed the male if it hadn't been for the cat.

Really, in this age of mass hysteria about the agents of evil, who was brave enough to walk around with a cat in tow? And not only that, the cat was huge, black, and definitely noticeable.

The second thing he noticed was the chains around the male's wrists, waist, and neck -- rather his corded waist, very thick wrists, and a neck that was exposed due to his lack of hair.

He didn't have a chance to contemplate this event further because his king, with a boding voice, bade him approach. He entered the audience chamber and ignored the massive set of silver doors that slammed shut behind him.

"I see you have returned to us from the realm of man." The king eyed him from the top of his tousled hair to his bare feet. "Unscathed?"

Vulwin nodded, standing tall before his king. "That I have, Your Shining Majesty." Vulwin wanted to smirk at the man, indeed he did, but common sense prevailed and he contained his amusement at this old familiar back and forth.

"Strip." The order was given negligently as the king turned to speak to one of his many advisors.

Vulwin looked around the chamber. Some things never changed. His king's pet crows still perched along the rafters of the dimly lit room. A mixture of candles and old fashioned gas lights gave the whole chamber a yellow tinge, while burning incense took away that odd smell that filled the chambers because of the gas lights.

This audience chamber was dominated by the

huge circular throne platform. It stretched along the back wall, its concave design dominating the small room. In the center sat the highest chair, the throne of the king, draped in furs and embroidered silks given as tribute from faraway lands. On either side of the throne sat two chairs, one for each of His Majesty's advisors who helped him maintain peace and order in the realms.

Knowing that he would be ignored until he complied, Vulwin let go of the human glamour he wore, his long, pale gold hair disappearing with a subtle flow of light, lengthening until it became the knee-length silvery white that helped lend him his second name, Valas -- silver in the old tongue.

As the light passed over his body, it took along with it his human skin tone -- the pale gold that humans called albino and that his human manager found attractive -- and in its place his natural skin bled through.

Valas was proud of his skin tone, black as the starry night with a tracery of brilliant stars that gleamed when the light hit it just so. Others called his complexion speckled, the mark of a blessed child, and with his easy life he tended to agree with those old tales. No one else in the realm had skin like his and he was proud to show it off, a little miffed that his current assignment had him hiding it from prying eyes, but content to be smug about it when he was summoned to make his periodic trips home.

Removing the glamour was but the first step. With a wave of earth magic, he conjured from the floor a low table that sprouted forth like a small tree. It grew to about waist height and then Vulwin began to carefully remove the jewelry that adorned his body, starting with the delicate chains and hoops of gold that swung daintily from his long, pointed ears.

Unlike other Fae, the Dhrovish could be identified in an instant from the long, arching ears that rose up majestically from the sides of their heads. It was a point of pride to sport the most perfectly arched ears and the Dhrovish adorned them properly to show off their shape. He knew that Elvhenkind often looked down upon the Dhrovish for their midnight complexions and their large, ungainly ears, but he thought they were overcompensating for their lack by harping on the subject. Besides, a good, large set of ears generally meant that the Dhrow was sporting something thick and meaty between his thighs.

Oh yes, Vulwin Valas had a massive set of ears.

The necklaces of gold followed and the many rings that adorned his fingers and toes were removed next. Then the human clothing was carefully pulled off and folded, the long tunic of black silk, the loose fitting pants, and the anklets with their tiny bells.

He wore no underpants -- he couldn't get used to that human concession -- so he stood there naked save for the thick swirl of ornate gold rings that encircled the base of his cock, his chastity device.

He stepped back from the conjured table and turned his gaze to his king. The man, still engaged in conversation with his advisors, motioned him forward with a wave of his hand.

Rolling his eyes at the apparent inattention, Vulwin stepped forward gracefully and paused a mere two human feet away from his king. Finally, the man paused in his conversations to eyeball his naked body.

Vulwin couldn't help but feel inadequate as the cool black eyes, shaped so much like his, passed over him in an almost dismissive fashion. He could feel the old feelings of being less, of feeling incomplete... of being a failure... surface once again. From the expression in his king's eyes, no matter what he did, he could never do enough, would never be enough, would always be lacking in some fundamental way.

Summoning up the experience of centuries, Vulwin managed to tamp down the reaction, hiding behind his usual indifference. At his side, his fingers twitched and he absently made a fist, the thumb on the inside pressed snugly against his palm. He squeezed, the comforting gesture beginning to settle his nerves.

"Turn," the king ordered, and obediently Vulwin gave a spin, showcasing his tall, lean, muscular form. With his true form revealed, he was a little too unearthly to be considered human -- his eyes, one silver and one black, a little too large, his limbs a little too long, his body too thick and corded with muscle in some areas and too delicate looking in others.

His shoulders were broad, and the right one carried a slight hunch of overly developed muscle, the body of an archer. His fisted right hand hid the many calluses he had developed while perfecting his craft, the pads of his thumb and main fingers hardened from pulling back on power-infused spider webs that he crafted to make his bowstrings. His thighs were thick with muscle used to hold crouched positions -- for hours, if need be -- on a hunt, or to cling to trees and buildings, finding the perfect angle for a shot.

These were all marks of a warrior tried and tested, blooded in battle, but within his king's eyes, all he saw was the need for improvement.

"Still a virgin, I see," the king commented as Vulwin completed his spin and faced the... not exactly damning, but maybe a bit disappointed gaze that traveled over his star-speckled skin. The silvery freckles of starlight didn't end at his face but rather trailed over his whole body, something unique to him and, as he'd learned, a trait of his long-dead mother.

"In some obvious places," Vulwin drawled, trying not to roll his eyes in annoyance, a purely human trait that would surely make that look of disappointment in his king's eyes grow deeper. "Your adornment has seen to that, Your Shining Majesty."

"Very good," the king said, as emotionless as ever.

As he watched his king watching him, he decided the man wasn't exactly emotionless. Anger and disappointment were two emotions, so the king wasn't a total dark pit of a being. "And you've made no attempt to remove them."

"The last attempt left me in so much pain I had to cancel two jobs I had lined up. I had to create some human stomach complaint and have the doctors at the hospitals heal me." That was an experience he never wanted to have again. And they came up with minor ulcers to explain the burns on his insides that the magic of the rings had caused. They admonished him to work less and rest more, like that was a thing in the modeling or assassination world.

"You are still taking pretty pictures for the humans?" his king asked, motioning him to step back, which he did gracefully. He almost felt naked without his jewelry, and although he knew it was just a prop to hide behind, he wanted his damn prop.

"I have to pay the bills somehow," he offered, smirking at his king. "And this gets me into areas where your glorious work can be handled discreetly while providing me an adequate alibi if the humans ever suspect me... which they haven't. So I guess that means I am successful at my assigned duties."

"No one ever questions your skill, my son," the

king spoke softly, only for his ears... and those of his advisors. "And you have ever been a loyal and dutiful subject."

Silence fell for a long moment while Vulwin examined his father. The king looked the same, eyes black as the midnight sky, a mere shade darker than his skin. His hair was still a silken fall that stopped easily at his ankles, the mark of a truly great warrior and a wise man, as only someone with intelligence and skill could function with that length of hair trailing behind him every step he took. He was as muscular as ever, as regal as ever, every gesture and movement of his body graceful as if he planned it before he took any action.

Yet something was wrong. His father, a stickler for protocol, brought to attention their blood connection. In this room there was no place for familial sentiment, as his father had driven into his mind from a young age. In this room they were king and subject and that was it until the appropriate time.

He was a *loyal and dutiful subject*? Why was his father offering him compliments? Something was really wrong. "Are you dying?" Vulwin asked, and all of the advisors turned to look at him, confusion on their faces. "Really? Have the Fae found a way to curse you that your -- that Kno can't counter?" He nodded to Kno, the advisor on his father's left, who stared at him with a blank face. "Have they? I have not fully obtained my maturity and it should be impossible to kill you before that, but have they found a way?"

"Vulwin." The king sounded... exasperated? Now he really was becoming apprehensive.

"Father." If the king was going to throw about blood connections then Vulwin felt justified in tossing out a few of his own. "What is going on?"

Calmly, his father responded and if Vulwin didn't know better, he would've sworn his father sounded amused. "I've had a boon granted to me from the very family of the Fae you recently exacted my vengeance upon."

There had been a murder on one of his father's outer lands recently, the killer clearly a Seelie Fae. The bastard had been so arrogant as to leave his arrows lying about the body. The victim was an older Dhrow whose son had recently obtained his full maturity, but instead of taking on the family business of jewel scribing, the son chose to become an explorer and open passages in newly acquired land to increase the wealth of his family's holdings.

The older Dhrow had been a master scriber and a genius silversmith in his own right. He had created some of the jeweled pieces that commonly adorned Vulwin's person and interacted in commerce and trade with humans and other preternatural beings as well. Wodnet Arvey was a Dhrow who easily straddled all worlds and was considered a neutral party when it came to political upheavals. Why the Dhrow was murdered, neither Vulwin nor his king could say despite an intense conversation, but several unique family heirlooms had gone missing.

Vulwin could easily track the killer, and with his king's permission, trailed him to where he had hidden amongst the humans with his stolen treasure. It was an easy matter to infiltrate his apartment and to bind the asshole in iron while he recovered what was stolen. The Elvhen Fae had begged for his life, but the Rule of the Dhrow stood in Vulwin's favor. In retaliation for the murder, the Fae's ears were removed and delivered to Wodnet's son, his abdomen split, his core filled with molten iron, and his remains sent back to the Fae's family, a warning of the blood price placed on his line.

After all, Wodnet was not just a master silversmith and jewel scriber, he was also of direct bloodline to the king through the five founders of the Dhrow.

"The Fae's family paid a blood boon to end hostilities between our line and theirs." Politics Vulwin understood, as they and protocol had been drummed into his head since he could speak his first words.

"Indeed they did, and a large boon it is."

"And have you discovered the reason Wodnet was taken from this world and ushered into the next realm?"

"A craving for things one could not obtain," the king answered.

"Father --"

"It was said that Wodnet possessed a Dragon Stone," Kno explained. Vulwin turned his eyes to his father's lover. "Like we would harbor such a thing."

"A Dragon Stone, you say?"

"One put into play by an ancestor close to The Five eons ago. It was rumored to be set in an ancient necklace, and after hearing tales of a slumbering Dragon, the young Elvhen Fae decided that it was the perfect lure to draw the Dragon out of his time to make him weak and vulnerable and then take possession of him."

"And why would someone want to, as the humans say, fuck with a Dragon? Dragon magic is nothing to play around with. They can end a life with a thought."

"An Elvhen life, yes." Kno, always one for showing emotion, chuckled at that. "Why those short-ears would mess around with a creature who can draw upon iron I will never understand, but yes, the young one wanted to capture a Dragon before his brother could, or so the rumors say."

The king nodded. "Foolish. Very foolish indeed. The Elvhish do not train sense and intelligence into their offspring. Instead they let them run catawampus all over the earth and in the realms. I remain amazed that they have not been discovered by the humans on the realm of man."

"So am I recognized as chosen Champion of the Line?" Vulwin mentally went over what he remembered about killing sneaky Elvhish Fae. He could easily defeat any warrior they threw at him, but he was never so arrogant as to believe that his victory would be an easy win. He would rather over prepare than to be caught short and harmed unnecessarily.

"Yes. As this was a direct affront to our line," his father contended. "It was an attack on the throne."

Vulwin had wondered if his father would ignore this aspect of the attack. Vengeance had been served on a personal level, but the political one, that could be acknowledged or ignored, and it appeared that something about this stirred more of his father's ire.

"So is it to be war?" Vulwin's body stiffened as he recalled the last Dhrovish- Elvhen conflict. The floors of the Gray Gulf had run green and silver with Elvhish and Dhrovish blood before the earth burned gray with death. It was true that a Dhrow could not be killed if his son had not reached full maturity, but that didn't mean they couldn't be maimed.

Vulwin had encountered several Dhrow who were cursed to a half-life with limbs missing and burned, head wounds so severe that they could scarcely be considered sane, and worst of all, warriors who had just obtained maturity purposefully castrated and forced to exist eternally as the undying, unable to procreate and gain the privilege of death while they waited for the madness of the void to consume them.

"No." The king turned his cold gaze to his son once more. "To prevent the Elvhen rulers from knowing fully what was done, the family has ceded to us their greatest treasure."

"A treasure grand enough to stop a righteous war of their own making and one powerful enough to prevent the end of a very foolish bloodline?" This treasure had to be something every ruler in the realms desired for his father to give up rightful blood thirst and lay down arms.

He was wrong when he thought his father only had two emotions; he'd completely forgotten his thirst to water his lands in green Elvhen blood.

"Indeed." The king smiled and Vulwin found himself taking an involuntary step back.

"And... what is this treasure?" he asked. "If it is proper for someone as lowly as me to know."

"As it concerns you, my son, I think it is entirely proper for you to know."

"Me?"

"Yes, my son. Rejoice, for the Elvhen have settled a matter that has long plagued me and left me concerned for your future."

"My future?" He didn't like where this was going. "Father --"

"Vulwin Valas, Prince to the Dhrovish throne, Walker of Two Worlds, the Silver Arrow of the King, the Elvhen have delivered unto you this day your mate."

Vulwin had to bite his tongue to hold back the only word that fit in this situation.

Fuck.

Chapter Two

"I don't want a mate."

"But you need one."

Vulwin turned away from his father and glared at the closed doors since he couldn't turn his agitated look upon his father without consequences. No one was deliberately rude to the king without action being taken, including his own son.

"And yet now is not the time to let this perfect opportunity slip through our grasp."

"Our grasp." Vulwin looked down at his clenched hands, rage battling with disbelief within him. He took a deep breath and tried to control the tensing of his muscles, the narrowing of his eyes, the snarl that was fighting to break free. When dealing with someone as stubborn as his father, he must remember to remain in control of his own emotions. "Why is this an opportunity?" He was trying to keep the rasp of anger from his voice and so far had succeeded in that, at the very least.

"Because human women don't dance in mushroom circles anymore, my son." The king snorted. "And from what you tell me of their advancing communications technology, if one were to disappear it would cause no end of problems as they have a habit of recording everything that they do for posterity and their viewers."

His father had a point and the thought of some perfectly contoured and coifed beauty tripping around on Louboutins in the center of a forest was kind of amusing. Rather than dance in the center of them, a lot of humans would rather pick the mushrooms and see if they could take them on a good trip. And then there were the ones who would record themselves and play with their confused mythology of the Fae people. God save him from wanna-be fairies.

"While that is true, My King," he allowed, as he turned to face his father again, "I don't see myself, to be blunt, fucking a short-ear to gain progeny. It would be a blood feud between our families when she died after childbirth, and the last time I checked, all of their human thralls were still under enchantment. If one stepped a foot out of their glorified mouse dens to even make it over the Gray Gulf, they would age into dust and dissipate before I could even touch her, let alone fuck her."

"I never said it was an Elvhen woman or an enthralled human female, Vulwin." The king looked at his son in a way that made his skin crawl. It was the same look he had on his face when he decided that Vulwin should learn about his mother's people -- for the good of the kingdom, of course -- and make his way out among the humans. Though he didn't regret his change in location now, he hadn't appreciated being cast off from his people at the time. He was an assassin, a Shadow of the King, a warrior tried and blooded in battle, not a diplomat or a spy. He'd learned to find his own way and had represented himself accordingly, but that look on his father's face always meant some dreadful change was being forced upon him. He'd learned to be wary of that look.

"Then who do you expect me to breed with, Your Shining Majesty? A pile of rocks? Maybe a troll? Oh, I know. They have found a way to duplicate me so that you can really tell me to go and fuck my --"

"Clear this room!"

Vulwin turned away from the look of growing anger on his father's face to his right where Kno, who had shouted the order, was on his feet and glaring at him.

Vulwin was so shocked that he remained quiet as the other advisors hastened to leave the chamber, leaving the three of them together alone in the charged silence.

After a pregnant pause, Kno placed his hand on the king's shoulder and his father visibly relaxed. The king huffed a bit at his lover, Kno, then turned to face Vulwin, the serious look in his eyes cooling Vulwin's anger.

"Will you allow us to explain?" Kno asked, taking his seat while keeping his hand on the king's shoulder. "It is very important, Vulwin. And I have a feeling that you will agree with your king's demands when you listen and absorb the facts."

"Absorb the facts," Vulwin grumbled, then nodded, pulling his pants from his pile of clothing and covering himself. "If this farce is going to continue, I need clothing. Being comfortable is conducive to understanding and understanding is half the battle."

"I feel the sarcasm in your words, my son," the king grumbled back. "But because I lack understanding I have no reason to pin back your ears."

"Tartran Sornaxel," Kno admonished, and his father huffed, crossing his arms over his chest.

"I am doing my best by the boy yet he will not heed his elder's advice."

"I'm still in the room," Vulwin pointed out, waving up a chair from the stone ground now that ceremony appeared to be tossed out the door. "You can speak directly to me, Your Shining Majesty. Please explain how saddling me with a mate of unknown origin is good for me and not just our shared bloodline or your kingdom."

"It will be your kingdom one day too, youngling.

You'd do well to remember that."

"Not in the next eon or so." Vulwin, with an effort, began to calm himself. "And it must be important because it got Kno to flex his muscles as first advisor."

"Flex his muscles…" His father tilted his head to the side as he examined his son. "Another human term, I believe? Maybe I allowed you to spend too much time in your mother's realm."

"They do have a colorful turn of phrase, Father," he allowed. "But these people aren't like my mother. Her time has come and gone hundreds of years ago. Time and custom do shift quickly on the human realm. I dare say you would scarcely recognize the place that my mother called home… or its people."

"That is something that the Dhrovishkind could never compete with and something that the Elvhen Fae try to emulate with some instances of success, though the change is hard on all of Faekind."

"And now that calm pleasantries have been exchanged, Kno" -- Vulwin nodded at the once again serene-looking man who always sat just to his father's right --"can someone explain what this change has to do with me and my so-called mate?"

"I have chosen the perfect mate for you, my son. I could have taken this Elvhen tribute and squandered it, yet I think of your future happiness."

"And my future happiness depends on me mating with some female who will undoubtedly pass after hours of torturous labor forcing my offspring from her belly?"

Vulwin forced himself to halt his hurtful words as he heard his father inhale sharply. Instantly he felt guilt as he threw the one thing in his father's face that was sure to cause him pain: the subject of his mother.

It was said that the Dhroven married once because of the pain of the loss of their mates, but all knew that to be a romantic myth said to ease the fears of the females unlucky enough to land in their realm. Dhrovish mated once because they were fearful creatures and loath to give their hearts to anyone they knew were going to break it... like the human mothers of their children.

Most Dhrow refused to give their hearts away, instead saving all their love for their sons, but his father, the high king, was the exception to the rule. He had fallen in love with his red-haired Scottish lass and spent centuries ensuring that their romping would not prove fruitful. Unfortunately, the Ladies Fate would have their way and his mate fell pregnant with the child who would not only steal her love from her husband but who would certainly die upon his birth.

From all the stories told, his father had fallen into a funk that lasted centuries, leaving others to care for his son. In fact, Vulwin's first memories of his father was some huge man with stunning white hair and black eyes yelling at him about his behavior after he beat down two of his age mates for stealing his toy swords. If he remembered correctly, he had been introduced to his father who immediately took him to task over his sword stance. That was one of the reasons that he'd kept his swordplay rudimentary and gravitated to the bow arts and became one of the fiercest archers ever to call the Gray Gulf home.

And now that very same man was speaking of his future happiness? There was a human saying that applied here. "Bullshit."

"Vulwin," Kno admonished, though his eyes twinkled in mirth. Vulwin knew that Kno was the one to read his weekly reports about humankind and summarized them for his father, who always appeared to be too busy with concerns of the realm to pay attention to what his castoff son had to say.

"My happiness, Father?" he asked the king. "How is it that you plan to ensure my happiness by securing me a mate?"

"I found you a mate who will not die."

The sardonic look on his face was enough to get his father's ire back to boiling.

"I repeat, I have found you a mate who will not die, youngling. I tell you of this wondrous news and you choose to stare at me as if I have gone insane."

"All of our mates die!" Vulwin all but screamed. "Every one. That is why there are so few females here, and they take the drug to prevent conception until they tire of their long lives."

"Humans are not designed to crave existence as we do," Kno was quick to explain. "But that is no reason to disbelieve what your father has to say. You no longer have to fear the loss of a mate."

"And is that why you, Kno of the Gray, have chosen never to take a mate but instead cling to the scraps of kindness that my father would offer in his great grief?"

His father started to rise, causing Vulwin to rise, as protocol that was drilled into him from the time he was young forced him to, but Kno placed a hand on his father's shoulder and the elder Dhrow subsided.

Without a word, Kno rose to his feet and the long silvery robes he wore as a sign of his position as head advisor and lover to the king fluttered to the ground like cherry blossoms, gently cascading down on an unfelt breeze.

Kno was a warrior in his prime. Tall and muscular, his skin taking on a rare gray tint that was responsible for his second name, he was even more muscular than Vulwin. Kno was a swordsman and it showed in his stance, the thick corded muscles in his shoulders and chest, in his straight posture and the thickness of his thighs that lacked the graceful flow of Vulwin's own. His hair, nearly ankle length and worn in braids, was tossed aside from its usual position over his left shoulder and his full naked body was exposed.

Vulwin let his gaze travel over Kno's body, nudity nothing to his people when they took pride in the war machines they forced their bodies to become. But his gaze stopped when they met with his groin.

Beneath his well-sized cock with its silver piercings and jewels lay... nothing.

Vulwin's eyes widened as his gaze turned toward Kno's face, words escaping him as he examined the face that was such a staple in his life. How could he not have known?

"It happened well before you were born, youngling." Kno spoke as he waved his hands and his robe flowed up his body, covering its strength and its tragedy once more. "In the last true Elvhen wars. My mate, who had a heroic fear of dying, decided to take matters of conception into her own hands. I was drugged, staked out, and castrated as neatly as if an Elvhen mage had cast the forbidden spell. I awoke without my ballocks and no wife, because your mother had discovered what she had done and decided to mete out her own vengeance as a friend and a claimed sister."

"Kno..." Vulwin paused. "I didn't realize --"

"And I didn't want you to." Kno took his seat beside Vulwin's father and tilted his head in his direction when the king placed a hand on his shoulder. "I am not ashamed of my half-life state, Vulwin.

Because I was castrated before I could produce a son, I will not die. I've had a mate I loved and then later despised. I say to you, take what your father is offering. It is a chance to get to know your mate, to discover who they really are before you give your heart or your hate away. With a partner who will not die you have options that the rest of us pray to the Ladies Fate for. Do not discount this gift because of your pride."

"Pride," Vulwin scoffed, but began to consider the advisor's words.

Kno had never, in all his years at his father's side, steered him wrong when it came to advice about life and his position in the king's household. And as long as the man would live, he had no reason to guide him into a life that would bring nothing but pain.

Was it really pride that was stopping him?

Vulwin knew that even though he had not been seeking out a mate, the thought of finding the human female he could spend centuries with concerned him. Okay, it terrified him. Human women were not what they seemed. In his industry, he could not see himself wanting to spend more than a brief dalliance with any of his female contemporaries. He took humanity on a case by case basis. Some examples were beautiful and taught him so much about life, yet a lot of them gave him appreciation for his skill as a warrior who could quietly take them out and then hide the bodies where they would never be found. He could not see himself choosing any of them to mate.

But his father's option... It would be one less thing for him to worry about. He could take the female with him and they could both live out among the humans, where his work in human guise and as an agent of the king would continue unhampered.

It would take a damn long time for his father to even consider passing along the throne, and in that time he could get to know the female and her ways. They could take their time and decide when and if they would reproduce. If plans did not work out, they could remain mated and yet go their separate ways until the draw of a child could not be denied. Then the female could go her own way and he could take care of his son the right way, devoting his love and all of his time to the one jewel in his life.

Though his father's plans had flaws, it also had merit.

"So." He finally looked over at his father. "What has His Shining Majesty procured for me for a mate? It is a good thing that we are not xenophobic and I have enough earth magic to cast a glamour over my chosen so I can bring her to the human world and still complete my job as your left hand."

He wondered if his mate would have tentacles. Tentacles would be fun. He had no objection to being penetrated, and crazy sex limbs would take eons to grow bored of.

"I am pleased that you are showing the sense and breeding I know you to have," his father intoned, sounding satisfied now that his royal plans were coming into fruition.

"My mate, father?" he prompted, rising to his feet and moving to stand in front of his king as he waved his chair away. "What is she?"

"I never said it was a she."

Now that threw him. What was his father playing at?

Before he could open his mouth to demand an explanation, his father grinned again, and this smile was one he had never seen before. It shot terror straight into the heart of him and caused him, a veteran of many battles, to take a step back. "A he, father? It does not work that way for Dhrow --"

"Neither a he nor a she."

Before his father could say more, there was a bellow, and something hard slammed against the audience chamber doors. There were screams and the shouts of his fiercest guard... and his father's smile grew wider.

"Neither a he nor a she, father?" he asked. "Did you procure me a hydra? Despite the legends saying that they are beautiful women --"

"Close, but no hydra."

"Father!"

There was another bellow and some screams and his father began to chuckle like an amused child. This was beyond the pale.

"Father --"

"I got you a Dragon."

Chapter Three

Iffear was bored... and horny. Really bored but definitely horny and growing more and more annoyed by the second.

He shifted his weight from one foot to the other and his familiar purred comfortingly, her black fur purposely flowing from her back and around the Elvhen warriors that surrounded him.

With a twitch of his nose, he set the flying hairs alight.

The screaming and yelling it caused made him not so bored anymore, but he was still horny and annoyed.

He had been fine; he had been sleeping this heat cycle away and maybe would venture out into human territory after his weeks-long nap when he felt the unmistakable draw of a Dragon Stone. In spite of his mind's best objections and his familiar's very vocal protests, he woke enough to follow its weak call to the entrance of his hidden den. The last thing he expected was an army of desperate short-ears circling and getting the jump on him in his weakened state. The magic-draining cuffs were just the icing on a very nasty cake and now he was nearly drained, forced along like chattel, and now dragged to a Dhrovish castle.

He really had nothing against the Dhrovish; indeed, they were pretty decent folk who kept to themselves and never tried to be anything other than what they were... unlike the vain Elvhen, who felt the need to stick their pointy noses and their obnoxiously colored skin into everything they saw. He was not feeling too charitable toward them at the moment as he stood in chains outside an audience chamber.

Setting Chinsie's spare hair on fire was more

than just something to do to alleviate boredom. It was a reminder that his magic could never be contained and was merely delayed until his heat cycle was over. Revenge was coming and it would be coming in hot.

He eyeballed the noble who stared back at him, concern on his face, while his guard rushed to beat out the fires he'd set. The Drovhen guards looked on in amusement. They liked fire. They liked anything compatible with earth magic and in this instance Dragon and Drovhen were definitely compatible... along with their almost obligatory general dislike of the Elvhen.

The noble gulped and backed away but made no effort to order his release. Something scared this brazen being more than the threat of Dragon fire and that fear had compelled him to drag him to the Dhrow.

What did you do, little man? He tilted his head to the side as the pale green creature blanched even more.

Bah. He would figure it out later. Right now, after his little display of magic, he was totally drained and wanted nothing more than to have a good fuck and go to bed. Heat season was not fun unless you had a comparable, stamina-driven mate waiting to serve you hand and foot.

He shifted his weight, making his chains ring out in deceptively delicate tingling tones, and one of the noble's guards, probably out of fear of more fire starting ruining their precious garb, jabbed him with a pike. It would haven't been any need for concern but two things happened. One, the guard shoved Chinsie out of his way to get to him, knocking her onto her side, and two, the bastard made him bleed his own blood.

Sure, nothing could really penetrate Dragon hide, but when in human form, their bodies were a lot more susceptible to Fae magic. Which is why they could get the chains around his body, which is why they could take him from his hidden mountain, which is why the short jab parted his skin and made his blood run down his arm. And of course, which is why his large familiar, Chinsie, now reared up and took on her battle size. Ordinarily she merely reached the center of Iffear's chest when she was on all fours.

But now, with a roar, she grew to the size of a small horse, with claws and lashing tail and teeth to match. She swatted the guard who had cut him and sent his body flying into the chamber doors with a loud *thump.* The dazed man's back collided hard enough to shake the walls and with his chest armor shredded, blood flowing like a river of green down his chest, he slid to the floor with a low groan.

"Wait!" the noble demanded but his guards were already on the move. They rushed Chinsie, who suddenly found something gleeful about this whole situation. She was now free to hunt.

She pounced at a second guard, who stood up to her determinedly with pike in hand. He jabbed upwards as the fellow guards divided into threes, a small group going to the fallen man at the door, a second surrounding the noble, and the third who now jabbed at his cat like she was an unthinking, mindless beast.

Again Iffear found his boredom lessening as he watched Chinsie deftly avoid being jabbed, twisting her body. Shutting her teeth around the wood of the bone below the iron head, she neatly bit it off. She landed on all fours before she tensed her body, tightened her muscles, and sprang once more. This time she swatted at the warrior's head, making him duck down and leaving the men behind him vulnerable to attack. She landed on his back, dug her nails in, rending flesh as she spring-boarded off of him and directly into the path of the oncoming soldiers, knocking them over as she dove for their knees, knocking them down like human bowling pins.

She threw back her head and screamed her victory as more Elvhen warriors converged and the Dhrovish guards stood back laughing, enjoying the show.

Iffear was seconds away from at least cracking a smile if not outright laughter when he felt the noble slip up beside him and place a cold iron knife against his throat. It was a testament to how exhausted and out of it he really was that the ponce was even able to slip behind him without him noticing.

"Call her off," he demanded, and Iffear slowly turned to peer at the man who stepped closer behind him, using him as a shield despite his many warriors. In the corner of his vision, he could see the pale green arm shaking, could smell the fear wafting off of the creature.

The man actually leaned further into him. The knife eased a bit from his throat, proving the noble's intentions not to do him any serious harm and unknowingly putting power back into Iffear's hands.

"Call her off," the noble demanded again and Iffear took great delight in rumbling at him, a curl of white smoke rolling up from his nose.

"No." He forced his jaw to work because even gathering up the energy to speak was a bit much with the magic-draining chains encircling him. His voice sounded rusty and disused even to his own ears, but that tended to happen when the last time you spoke out loud had been months ago.

At this point, Iffear really couldn't care less what

was happening. His heat was growing worse, the pangs tearing at his stomach and turning his thighs to water, and he was feeling tired and drained. If they were going to kill him then they needed to get on with it. He was finding it harder and harder to care.

That was the danger of separating the magic from the being at such a delicate time. His magic was central to his survival and continuation of the species. And when that drive to live was cut off, the being found his will to exist slowly draining away. Iffear was nearly to the point where he would have happily died just to end the torment of being cut away from his will to live and his magic. But if it was going to happen, then he would go to the next life taking great pleasure in foiling this asshole's plans.

Chinsie, upon hearing his voice and seeing the blade against his neck, let loose a howl that vibrated the stone walls and even made the Dhroven guards flinch. The noble winced, cutting into Iffear's skin, then began to babble as Chinsie ignored the warriors trying to circle her and crouched, her tail lashing, her eyes intent on the small cut on his neck.

"He will pay in blood!" Her mental shout echoed in the waiting area and the watching Dhrow guards leaned in closer, anxious to see the spilling of green blood on gray stones.

The noble began to whimper, but before either party could make a move, the doors swung open and a tall, lithe form stomped barefooted through the entranceway.

The Dhroven guard at once stood at attention as a spark of earth magic filled the air.

That caught Iffear's attention and made his body take notice. His magic, as bound as it was, thrummed at the lightning feel of the man.

This Dhrow sparked with life and power, with an energy that made Iffear want to just lean against him and take it all in. His hair was a waterfall of silvery white silk though he knew from past experience that Dhrow hair was a lot more wiry than it looked. His shoulders were broad and muscular, his forearms corded and hard looking. His skin was solid black and velvety with silver sparkles as if he had been sprayed with moon dust. His ears were long and thick, wrapped in threads of gold, the same gold that encircled his fingers and his toes. His face was androgynous and beautiful, oval shaped with a slightly pointed chin and high cheekbones. But it was his eyes that were the most arresting. One was the deep black of the night sky and the other shimmered with all the majesty of the moon. He moved with grace and elegance, his glance around the room taking in everything at once before settling on him... Well, not on him exactly, but the seeping blood from the nick on his neck and the shaking, green-tinted hand that held the blade that had cut him.

He hissed and even the Dhrovish guard flinched as the Elvhen warriors fell back, looking none too certain about their actions.

Suddenly, Iffear found himself becoming amazingly, and probably inappropriately, amused and aroused.

* * *

"What goes here?" Vulwin snapped out the Elvhen words with as much disdain as he could muster... and looking at the sorry group he now faced, it wasn't hard.

There were Elvhen warriors everywhere, some surrounding the now larger-than-man-size cat, some tending to a fallen short-ear who was bleeding green all over the nice clean floor, and another group surrounding a shaking nobleman and what could only be *his* Dragon.

His eyes narrowed in anger because his Dragon was now bleeding from two places, wounds that hadn't been in place when he'd passed by them earlier.

The knife arm dropped instantly and the Elvhen noble was suddenly falling all over himself to bow.

"Your Shining Majesty --"

"Do I fucking look like my father?" the Dhrow snapped out and watched as the lower lord went over mental protocol to see where he had fucked up in his introduction.

"Excuse me, My Lord --"

"Your Highness or just Prince," he gritted out, not in the mood for political stupidity when it came to protocol. "I am not my father. I have no idea what you call your own crown prince, but to gift me with the title reserved for my father is treason, or in the case of foreign dignitaries, disrespect."

The noble gulped and nodded, the knife disappearing into the folds of the long cloak he wore. Then Vulwin turned to speak to his guards.

"I believe I asked a question..." He trailed off.

The noble gulped and stepped closer to him and his guard instantly reacted, drawing glaives of cold iron in preparation to defend their prince.

"Your Highness," the noble began to speak, looking with concern at the guard, "let us be reasonable."

"How can I be reasonable when I don't even know what is going on here? I smell burned hair of cat, I see a being leaking blood that he was not leaking before, and I see my guard reacting as if you are a threat. Won't someone please rid me of my confusion?" The words were softly spoken but carried a lot of weight.

He turned to his guard before the noble could speak, and instantly he was given a concise and accurate report.

"The captive being ignited hair from what appears to be his familiar. The Elvhen guard of Lord Claddafin the Bold attacked him, drawing his blood with a pike."

"Now wait --" But Vulwin threw up a hand and the outraged noble fell silent.

"The familiar," the guard carried on as if the short-ear had not even spoken, "reacted and drew rightful blood against the one who had harmed him."

"This is an outrage..." This time Vulwin turned his complete attention to the Elvhen noble and again the man stopped, taking one step back as his warriors moved closer around him.

"Interrupt again," Vulwin stated plainly enough, "and I will split your tongue and remove half of it for your impertinence. You had your chance to speak and you didn't take it. Now remain silent."

He turned back to his guard who continued with his report.

"When the familiar sought his justice, the Elvhen warriors" -- the guard almost choked on that word -- "divided; a force went to the fallen warrior, a force went to attack the familiar, and a force went to protect the... uh... lord. When the cat went on the defensive and removed several warriors from their feet, the lord drew a blade on the bound captive and demanded he rein in his familiar. The captive refused and was injured. Its familiar was about to retaliate for the second blood drawing when you arrived, My Prince."

Vulwin turned his attention to the Elvhen noble,

who looked pale under his green-tinted skin. "So you have a defenseless captive that you drew blood from twice. How fearful this captive creature must be."

His guard tittered in amusement, their laughter sounding like the chirping of cats, as he took a step closer to the noble and his captive, his guards following, glaives still exposed.

"There is no need for weapons, Your Highness," the noble began.

"You drew blood twice on a bound captive. I don't think my guard trusts you around me, an unarmed male, in your presence."

"I would never --" he paused.

"Yet you already proved that you and your people would... twice."

The noble went limp, his flaxen mane of hair losing its shine. "He is meant to be an offering to your line --"

"Because someone, and from the look of you, I'd say one of your sons, decided that murder was a way to get what he wanted when negations failed. You reared such a creature and let it loose upon the world and now you offer up the freedom of another to banish the sins from your bloodline and your king."

The noble began to look scared and that only made Vulwin's guard titter more even as the Elvhen warriors moved in closer to defend their charge.

"I would not word it as such --"

"Because if word got back to your king that your people, your blood, your son nearly destroyed the hard-won peace created by flowing rivers of green and silver blood, he would see to it personally that your whole line, a part to his folly or not, would cease to exist in this world."

The Elvhen noble swallowed hard at this and

offered a shaky nod. "It is as you say, Your Highness."

"No explanations for the actions of your direct and close blood kin?"

"The youngling was not ready for society."

"The youngling was older than I by a century at least," Vulwin countered. "I know because I had a long conversation with him before I gutted the coward and gave his ears over to my cousin in recompense for the loss of his beloved father's life."

There, *that* was a flash of anger in the noble's face as he stared aghast at Vulwin, and Vulwin himself welcomed any action the man would take. He wanted him to do something, *anything*, that would allow him to remove this stain from the face of the earth. His kind made him sick -- spoiled, pampered soft men who claimed warrior status by right of birth rather than being blooded in actual combat. And his son had been no better, hiding out amongst the humans until things "blew over" and he could safely return without his prize but with Dhrovish jewels as compensation for his wrong. This was just one of the many reasons the Dhrovish people abhorred the Elvhen.

"As recompense..." The noble spoke now with a sterner voice and Vulwin could not imagine how it would feel to stand before an enemy hated for years and have to apologize and offer tribute after discovering the one you're begging favor from is the one who murdered your child. Of course, Vulwin and his people didn't view it as murder, but for a grieving father... "I offer you the life of this being, to do with as you will."

Vulwin turned to look at the being and considered him, then shot the noble the same disgusted look he gave the captive. "A battered, injured being whose life you are trading and not of your own?"

"My line has offered enough blood in sacrifice for our perceived wrong."

"Perceived wrong, huh?" Vulwin drawled, taking a step closer to the noble who stared defiantly up at him. "Perceived when yours invaded neutral ground, murdered kin to the royal house, and stole from his coffers? How is this only a perception of wrong, pray tell me?"

The noble opened his mouth and Vulwin spoke right over him.

"And to correct this wrong and prevent a blood feud, you offer me a life that is not your own, the life of a being who has no connection to you at all, am I correct?"

"But --"

"Am I correct?" he roared, and the iron in the noble's spine melted away.

"That would be correct, Your Highness but --"

"But?" He stepped closer and a wave of his arms had the man's warriors brushed aside by an invisible wind. *"But?"*

"It is a Dragon."

Vulwin smiled. Sometimes politics was fun.

"So you magically bound poorly -- and I say poorly because it was able to perform enough magic to burn free-flowing hair and its familiar is still powerful." He nodded at the cat, which was slowly shrinking back to its original size and smiled as it nodded in return. "You compound this by wounding the being who you have enslaved and then offer it to me, a wounded Dragon who will no doubt try to murder you before he turns his ire on my house as soon as I remove those chains."

"No, Your Highness," the Elvhen noble was

quick to deny.

"No?" Vulwin sneered. "Then you obviously know nothing about the nature of Dragons."

"This particular Dragon was lulled from his den from a deep sleep, Your Highness."

"There is only one thing that will pull a Dragon from his sleep --"

"I possess a Dragon Stone, Your Highness," the noble explained before lifting up a jeweled necklace he wore, exposing a glittering red stone in its center. "Nothing else will lure a Dragon from its sleep."

"So you refused to let sleeping Dragons lie and compounded your offense by dragging part of his ancestors along with you."

"Ancestors?" Now the noble looked confused, his glee receding a bit. "Ancestors, Your Majesty?"

"A Dragon Stone is the embryo plucked from an immature egg, you dolt. You are waving around the corpse of its ancestor like it is some prize opal."

The Elvhen pulled the necklace from his neck, staring at it in horror.

"It was what your son was after, listening to the rumors that my cousin possessed one. My people would never disrespect another living being so."

"I didn't know --" he began but Vulwin waved him off.

"It would take more than that to lure a sleeping Dragon. What else did you do?"

"This is all that is needed --"

"No. That is all that is needed to drive a Dragon into a killing rage. What did you do?"

"Nothing, I swear! Nothing! It is the time of year when unmated Dragons take to their dens for sleep because they fall into heat."

"Ah." Vulwin nodded. "That is what you did.

You drew a Dragon in the midst of sleeping through a heat -- two times when they are the most vulnerable -- out of his den by waving around the body of a dead child."

The silence that fell was almost physically felt and damn heavy.

Vulwin turned his gaze upon the Dragon, who stared at him before blinking very slowly once.

"So I'm going to tell you what I'm going to do," Vulwin began, stepping close enough to rip the necklace from the short-ear, tearing the chain as he carefully cradled the jewel in the center. "I am going to do this much to protect and save us... well, me and mine. I will accept your offer of this life..." He turned to the Dragon. "But not as chattel. This Dragon will become my mate and thereby by binding, become a member of the royal line. Then I will remove his chains, and what a royal member of the direct bloodline to the throne decides to do with his freedom and his returned magic, I haven't a clue."

The noble looked ready to pass out. The smell of his fear was almost overpowering.

"I could take what you offered to be a death threat against my whole line, that you attempted to benignly wipe us out of existence. I could assume that is what you meant by offering us a wounded Dragon you taunted and teased so much. But instead, I am going to look at this as a blessing, a boon to add to my line's strength and power, the joining of earth and fire magics."

He turned to the Dragon, noting how those fierce red eyes were figuratively glued to his face. "Do you accept?" he asked, and the Dragon nodded once.

"Then I accept your prize."

The Dragon sneered at the noble. A flash of

white light surrounded both Vulwin and the Dragon, their words creating an instant mating bond.

"Beautiful." Vulwin whispered it.

Before the noble could say anything, a wave of Vulwin's hands snapped the magical chains binding the Dragon's magic. They shattered into a thousand shards, all of which suddenly paused in midair before flowing towards the noble. The gasps of pain were almost as exciting as seeing the tiny shards embed themselves in the noble's body, small trails of green blood flowing out to paint his skin.

"Now that my mate is free I suggest you... run."

With the Drovish guards' chittering laughter in the background, the Elvhish warrior turned and fled, his guard behind him as Vulwin turned lazy eyes to his new mate.

"Do you have anything to say?" he asked as its familiar shrank to the size roughly of a human kitten and began weaving in and about between the Dragon's legs.

"One thing." Its voice was a deep rumble from lack of use if it was lured from a dead sleep.

"And that is?"

Vulwin blinked, and as if by magic, the Dragon was in his face, his red eyes blazing with something that could only be described as fierce hunger.

"Fuck me."

Chapter Four

It took everything in Vulwin not to give in to the demands of his mate and take him right there before the guards and all of sundry. But there were two things staying his hand. One, he would never disrespect his mate by coupling in full view of others. If others were invited to attend that was one thing, but outright rutting before the audience hall -- that was something that was completely beyond the pale. Second, there was the matter of that golden band that encased the base of his cock. One could not fuck if one could not get it up.

That was the problem with magical chastity items. They could give the illusion of the ability to fuck and frolic as you pleased but the reality was that illusion was all you got.

Vulwin's human lovers, male and female, had pulled, sucked, and played with his fully hardened cock to the point he thought his head would explode. Yet the moment penetration was attempted, he would fall, well, limp and flat. To prevent that embarrassment after the first few attempts, it was known that Win Rover was a confirmed bottom with both men and women and could quite frankly kick your ass if you wanted to make an issue of it.

He was by no means a virgin, yet there was one small thing that he hadn't been able to achieve thanks to his father's family planning. And to actually achieve that one thing, he would need his father's help.

Sucking in a deep breath, he pulled his gaze from the bright flame-red eyes of his new mate and gave himself an all over shake.

"We must seek my father," he forced from his dry throat as his mate was suddenly just... on him.

Oh Fates, was it on him... There was a well-muscled chest pressed against his own; two large, rough hands gripping his shoulders, sliding down his back... and there was a set of full, damp lips pressing into his neck, sharp teeth nipping at his neck, and a deep, gravelly voice murmuring into his suddenly very sensitive skin... "Fuck me now."

"I -- I don't... your name," Vulwin managed to stammer as his Dragon mate, who happened to be quite a bit shorter than him, gave a leap and then two thick thighs were wrapped around his waist. "Oh, fuck --"

"Iffear," it purred. "I gave you something, now it's time you give me something... like your dick. Fuck me now!"

Vulwin didn't know exactly when his hands dropped to cup one of the tightest, fullest, roundest asses he had ever beheld, but they were now on Iffear's rear, holding him in place as he tried to figure out what to do next.

Arousal was tearing at him so badly he could barely stand upright. His palms were sweating, his nerves zinging with electricity, and his cock...

The flesh was willing but the magical chastity-maintaining cock ring was strong. He was as limp as a wet noodle, although his balls were tight and his cock was more than ready to be sunk into some hot, wet Dragon flesh.

He opened his mouth and the sound that emerged was more of a whine than a groan, but it was all that he could do as he stood there cradling his mate in his arms, trembling like some untried youth, and wishing for something to happen to ease the ache in his belly and his balls. But his father's blasted...

"Father," he gasped as he spun around to face

the audience chamber doors.

Ignoring the snickers from his guards, he hopped, shuffled, stepped over to the doors while carrying his hot, begging... begging... mate in his arms. Luckily enough one of the laughing guards kindly decided to hold in some of his laughter to open the doors for him.

"Thanks," he muttered, then closed his eyes as his mate began to grind his hard cock into his stomach, his strong legs holding him in place while the kisses and bites traveled down to his neck and shoulders.

Iffear was going to kill him.

He managed to make it before his father before the sound of his tunic tearing filled the silence in the room, making his excited groan all the louder when Iffear attached himself to a nipple and began to lick it like it was the sweetest treat he had ever tasted.

"So, the courting goes well, my son?" King Tartran asked as Kno, still beside him, began to outright laugh in his face.

"Ob -- obviously, Your Shining -- Ouch, no biting," he admonished a glassy-eyed Iffear before looking up to his father once more. "Your Shining Majesty."

"Having... issues, my son?" How that bastard could look so smug and commanding at the same time, Vulwin would never know.

"None whatsoever, Your Majesty," he managed to speak without stumbling over his words or humping at his mate. "But there is a boon I must request of you."

"Really?"

Bastard! Iffear was now nipping at his ear and he felt his knees shake. His Dragon smelled of earth and loam and fertile things and it was driving him out of what was left of his mind. Never had he been hit with arousal so powerful and strong for a being he'd barely even met. It had to be the mate bond between them and it was powerful. Silently he wondered if any of his Dhrow ancestors had ever been left with the same problems, and... Was his mate's heat driving him into rut?

He narrowed his eyes at his father. And his laughing lover, Kno, could at least try to be a little more subtle in his amusement! He wanted to really just punch him once -- just once -- in the face.

"If his Supreme Majesty so... wishes --" Damn it, his Dragon was grinding his hips again in the most delicious circles, the thickness of his swollen cock a heat that couldn't be ignored. How big were Dragon cocks anyway? He might want to be fucked but Iffear had better get it in his head that he was going to have to give up some dick in this relationship too. Why should Vulwin be doing all the work all the time and miss out on... that. "I would like to request the removal..." He had to pause and close his eyes as Iffear's scent grew more powerful and the other half of his tunic was torn from his body.

"Fuck yeah," Iffear muttered before attaching his lips to Vulwin's other nipple, making him stumble and nearly fall on his face in front of his father.

Kno was nearly lying on the floor, his laughter was shaking his body so hard. His father was looking more and more pleased with himself and the royal guard no longer could stifle their snickers. This was beyond the pale, even for him.

"Damn it, get this stupid ring off of me!"

"So I am to assume that you want the removal of the --" his father began, only to be cut off by Vulwin as some of his hunger turned into anger.

"Get this damn ring off of me now so I can go and fuck my mate!"

"Rather forcefully done, Highness." Kno broke off laughing hard to snort at him.

"Not yet," Iffear growled, paying no attention to protocol.

"Will you not introduce us?" The king was a dick. Really, that's what went through Vulwin's mind -- that and imagining what his mate would be like without those leather pants...

"My mate, His Shining Majesty, Tartran Sornaxel, Two Thousandth in the Line of Allbright, King of all United Dhroven lands. Father, my Dragon. Now please --" He bit off the word, threw back his head, closed his eyes, and hissed as Iffear's wandering hands discovered his ass and how much fun it was to play with it... "Please remove this ring."

"You don't seem to be able to remove your pants."

"Father!"

"You've teased the young one long enough." Kno had finally stopped laughing, though he was smiling at Vulwin in a way that made him decidedly nervous. "Just remove the magic and let the young prince go."

"I don't think either of them are good for conversation right now," the king mused as Vulwin glared harder. "Fine."

Tartran chuckled and waved his hand.

The wave of power that rushed over them even gave Iffear pause as he pulled his mouth away from feasting on his mate to look at the sitting monarch.

But for Vulwin, his knees buckled as the rush of energy traveled from his bare feet up through his body. The powerful earth magic stole his breath and sent his mind reeling as the chastity power in the ring suddenly was no longer holding him back.

Vulwin screamed as his cock swelled to its fullest between his thighs and years of repressed desire slammed into him all at once. Then a release rolled over him, so intense his knees buckled.

His back arched as he toppled backwards onto the ground, his hold on his Dragon slipping as his hands flew outwards, clutching at earth which only increased the power of his orgasm. His balls burned and his cock jerked as his seed exploded from his body, tearing screams from his throat as his vision whited out.

It seemed to go on forever before the power began to wane and he slowly regained control of his body. First, he became aware of the weight of his Dragon pressing him down and his arms automatically wrapped around him, anchoring himself to Iffear as his body shook through the final throes of his release. Next, he noticed the slick, cooling stickiness that plastered his pants to his thighs and cock... And his cock... It had never been so sore, so throbbing, and still hard enough to crack a diamond between his legs.

He opened his eyes and a pair of bright red orbs stared back down at him. He couldn't even work up the energy to blush. There was silence in the chamber. The only real noise was his staggered breathing as his body spasmed for the last time before his muscles tried to slide off his bones and delve back into the earth from which they were made.

"Well." After several moments the king's voice broke the quiet in the room. "That happened --"

Vulwin tore his eyes away from those of his mate to glare at his amused father... who wisely closed his mouth and stared back as he threw up his hands in the universal sign of *I am unarmed, don't kill me.*

The sound of low, hissing laughter drew his eyes back to Iffear's. "If that was foreplay," he purred as he dropped his head to Vulwin's neck, settling himself comfortably as Vulwin realized that the hard column of his cock was now gone and replaced by the Dragon's scalding hot release against his stomach, "the sex is going to kill me."

Vulwin groaned, dropping his head back onto the earth as Kno's laugher once again rang throughout the chamber. Sometimes, he really hated his life but for now, he was trying to figure out how he was going to peel them both off of the ground with what dignity he had left and make it back to his quarters.

* * *

It was a race to get back to his rooms at the palace, a race that had to be witnessed by the guard who cleared the path to those rooms but had enough decency not to stare at the huge damp patch decorating the front of his pants.

It was a curious parade that wound its way through the dark stone halls of the royal palace, snickering guards who were looking dead ahead and not staring at their prince, a rather large cat who stalked along with them, hissing at nobles, servants, and anyone who dared catch a peek as the spectacle passed, and finally in the middle, a whimpering prince who carried a growling, smoking Dragon in his arms.

With both of the Dragon's legs wrapped around Vulwin's waist, Vulwin was amazed that he could even move as his mate's hard cock jammed wetly against his stomach with his every move.

Finally, they made it to his suite and the guards scattered when they entered and the cat, Chinsie, began to explore the rooms.

"I think we need a bath," Vulwin explained to Iffear.

"I think I need to get fucked and you are being stingy with the dick."

That made Vulwin's right eye twitch as he looked up at his mate, who had gone from lapping at the sensitive skin of his neck to staring down at him with glaring red eyes.

"I want to get us clean."

"Why? We are just going to wind up dirty."

Vulwin glared up at him, amused despite himself. "You seem very coherent for someone in the throes of a heat."

"I am in heat, not brain-damaged." Iffear sniffed. "Besides, I am freshly mated. I want to have sex with my mate. It's a good way to advance one's knowledge of the partner one has chosen."

"That is true," Vulwin agreed. "But I'm afraid I'll need a few moments to recover myself after... uh..."

"After Daddy's magic made you spew like a geyser? That was kind of incestuous..."

"Hey!" Vulwin warned. "Don't go there."

"So do you and your daddy --"

"He is my *father* and no, we really don't go there. I hear that has happened before in royal lines, Elvhen royal lines, but nothing like that occurs in *my* bloodline. I am connected directly to the original five, the band of war brothers who established the Dhrow nation. We don't have time for father-fucking. We're too busy keeping the peace."

"So what was that about?" There was no judgment in Iffear's eyes. He was genuinely curious.

"I -- I spend a lot of time in the human realm."

"Amazing. So do I." Iffear grinned, and it was all teeth that appeared sharp enough to shred even tough

Dhrow skin. "My main residence, if you will. Please, go on."

"Well, I am my father's shadow. You need to know that right off the cuff, my mate. I am an assassin."

"And you kill those who flee into the human world for safety, as there has never been a Dhrow sighting there."

"Correct." Vulwin shifted his mate's weight and nodded, pleased with his quick grasp of the situation. "You're very smart."

"I am highly intelligent, observant, and older than you. And I still don't understand the orgasms with magic. If that is a Dhrovish thing, I need to be made aware that if each time your daddy does magic around you, it's going to be clean up on aisle three."

"You have a great grasp of human idiom."

"I should," the Dragon said. "I am a tattoo artist in the human realm. I spend more than enough time around them putting them in willing pain for the art they want and I hear some of the most creative language humans have ever devised. I understand them. So, your daddy's magic? Permission and some kind of ring... explain."

"My father, in all of his great wisdom, decided I would be too busy chasing ass and pussy to do my job, so he slapped me in a chastity ring before I was banished to the human realm."

"And how long have you been up there?"

"Two hundred years."

"Whoa," Iffear breathed, his eyes widening in surprise at hearing that. "Two hundred --"

"Before then I was in and out, taking my missions and then returning here. About two hundred years ago my father wanted me to remain there and return home for the occasional inspection."

"I have never felt Dhrow magic and I have been out amongst the humans for a thousand years."

"Maybe we don't move in the same circles," Vulwin decided, shifting Iffear's weight and moving them toward the bathroom. His pants were clammy and cold, he was getting tired of standing in one spot, and he could feel his cock stir in interest with the amazing scent his mate was putting forth. Bath and then bed... or maybe bath and fucking in the bath. Either way worked for him.

"What do you do?" Iffear asked, unable to hide his curiosity.

"I model."

Iffear blinked twice, tilting his bald head to the side. "Have I ever heard of you?"

"I am known as Win Arcarious."

"The black albino model!" Iffear bounced in joy at the discovery. "You're big news, my mate. This is amazing. But how, if you are so noticeable, can you sneak up on Fae?"

"I have my manager plot jobs in the area where the soon-to-be deceased would be spotted. Trust me, humans see what they want to see. I can be on the job, on a runway or a shoot, take a break, pop into the guise of someone else, off my subject, and be back before they notice I have gone. The more I stand out, the more safety I have to do my job."

"Yes." Iffear nodded sagely as they entered the bathroom, and a wave of Vulwin's hand had a huge marble tub filling with hot water. "They would notice a tall albino with blond hair roaming around stabbing people, but if the last time they saw that tall albino, he was in his trailer taking a constitutional, then that is what everyone would see. You would be able to move around in anonymity. Brilliant."

"I thought so." Vulwin grinned up at his mate.

"But that doesn't explain the cock ring."

"Chastity device," Vulwin growled. "It appeared at one point Father thought I was getting too frisky with the ladies and the gents so I had this thing slapped on me when I took up residence, and since then --"

"You haven't been able to get it up. Am I going to shock you with my overt and demanding sexuality, Vulwin?"

Vulwin felt his cock lurch as his mate said his name for the first time. It rolled off his tongue, his accent strange to his experienced ears. Was that a Dragonish accent?

"Uh, no." Vulwin made a move to put his mate down but Iffear righted his grip with his legs. He wasn't going anywhere anytime soon. "I assure you, nothing you can do will startle me."

"So you haven't -- In two hundred years --"

"Win Arcarious is known as a hungry power bottom, my mate, begging for it most days."

"But you never --"

"The ring prevents me from entering another person, Iffear. I still got my rocks off. I just haven't sunk into anything tight, soft, and wet in many years."

Giving up on getting his mate off of him, Vulwin used a bit of earth magic to wave his pants away. Where they landed, he didn't really care. He all but dove into the hot water and sighed as it began to loosen muscles he didn't know were tense.

"Anal orgasms, then?" Iffear looked very understanding.

"That's right. I haven't shot a load in two hundred years. The humans think I have a kink but

they have a wild time and I get my release that way."
Vulwin sank back against the rounded ledge of the tub
and closed his eyes in pleasure. "But that was the first
ejaculation in over two hundred years."

"And you are still conscious?" Iffear snickered
and Vulwin opened one eye to glare.

"I mean that as a compliment to your stamina,"
the Dragon said and chuckled. "I myself would have
curled up and gone to sleep right on that floor."

"In front of your king?" Vulwin teased.

"The Dragonish have no king." Iffear sniffed, the
hold of his legs relaxing a little as he began to run wet
hands over his mate. Vulwin purred in agreement of
his new arrangement, his own hands taking the time to
do a bit of wandering as well. His Dragon was well-
muscled and yet had the softest skin.

"You do now, Prince," Vulwin teased and Iffear
groaned. "That's what you get for mating with a
prince. You now share my title."

"Great," Iffear grumbled, smoke rolling from his
nose. "After all these years, locked into responsibility."

That made Vulwin laugh as he ran his hands up
his mate's back, feeling the lines and groves of... scars?
He really hadn't paid attention at the time, but he was
paying attention now. "Did they harm you?" His
hands pressed harder against Iffear's back as he sat up.

"What? Oh, no." Iffear shook his head, giving his
mate a grin, probably at the sudden streak of
protectiveness he was showing. "What you're feeling
are the lines of my tattoo."

"You have a tattoo?"

"Wouldn't be a trustworthy tattoo artist without
one," Iffear explained, chuckling. "It's part of my
human guise."

"It just occurred to me that I don't know much

about you at all," Vulwin said, settling back in the water, his desire for Elvhen blood dying as fast as it had ignited. "Tell me something."

"What do you want to know?"

"Do you identify yourself as male or female? You're a Dragon. You choose your own gender."

"I'm male. So when you knock me up, I will be a fat male until I push your child out."

"I thought Dragons laid eggs," Vulwin said, suddenly feeling right stupid.

"You know about Dragon gender but not about reproduction?"

"It's not like you guys hand out books," Vulwin grumbled as Iffear threw back his head in laughter. "Give me a break."

"I would have a live birth for you, My Dhrow, because of your nature. If I got pregnant again, and that is a huge if, I would lay an egg. Dhrow breed true yet so do Dragons. You would have your Dhrow son because of your nature. I would lay my eggs and they would create Dragonlings because that is also in my nature."

"I -- well, then." Vulwin was suddenly taken with the thought of a little dark-skinned Dhrow tugging at his pants, staring up at him with bright red eyes. For a moment he began to understand the drive to reproduce that other Dhrow in their maturity spoke of with reverence and trepidation. He could get his mate pregnant, but the bonus was that it wouldn't kill him. That right there completed the mission of getting his cock fully hard and eager.

"That makes you happy, Dhrow?"

"That I can get you pregnant and not kill you in the birthing? That makes me very happy, yes."

"So does this mean we can get to the baby

making now? Heat drives us to want to mate, and it is uncomfortable. But it doesn't make us stupid if it's sated. Vulwin, I feel my IQ dropping."

Vulwin threw back his head, his laugher echoing in the humid room as he peered through the steam at his mate. Then he found his laughter coming to an abrupt end as his mate reached between them and gripped his cock, hard.

Iffear was done playing. His Dragon tightened his fist around his mate's hard length and Vulwin whimpered. He couldn't be arsed about the strange sounds his Dragon was pulling from his throat with such ease because he couldn't remember the last time he'd felt anything so good.

His toes were tingling and the muscles of his thighs shook. His hands went to his mate's shoulders, his fingers trailing down the firm skin of his back as his hips arched helplessly.

"This is what I want." Iffear bent closer to him, his tongue tracking along his lips, and mindlessly Vulwin opened his mouth and invited him in.

The flavor of his mate, musk and spice and something sweet that could only be Iffear, exploded within his mouth. His Dragon's long tongue danced with his, slick and hot, before it began to trace his sharpened eyeteeth and the warm cavern of his mouth.

Vulwin went to return the exploration but Iffear pulled back. "Teeth," he whispered. "They are sharp."

"And Dhrow are tough." He reached up and gripped his mate's head between his hands before he took over the kiss, dominating his Dragon's mouth.

Iffear let out a whimper, and Vulwin could feel Iffear's cock like a hot club pressed against his belly as he invaded his mouth. Almost as if the pleasure was too much to take, Iffear writhed on his lap as Vulwin ran his tongue over his Dragon's very sharp teeth.

He was so hot and solid on his lap. Vulwin spread his legs further to balance him as Iffear began to grind against his stomach. The kiss broke and he opened eyes he didn't even realize he'd closed to look up at his red-eyed mate.

He looked desperate, his skin flushed red, and low growls were rolling from his throat. Iffear's grip on his cock never loosened and now he was gently stroking him, petting him, toying with the filigree of the golden ring that still encased the base of his cock. Vulwin's hips were thrusting into his hands even as his control broke.

He exploded from the water, his mate in his arms, and all but ran to the bed. Iffear was placed carefully in the middle of his huge bed, the white pelts on his bed absorbing the water as Vulwin looked over his mate.

"You're beautiful," he purred as Iffear spread his legs and showed him where he needed him the most.

His Dragon's nipples were peaked and bright red, his stomach a washboard of muscle. His fingers were petting the fur beneath him as he writhed on the bed, the contrast between his tan skin and the white pelt stunning. His face was beautiful, his chin strong and his cheekbones high, his eyes twin orbs of burning red.

Iffear's body... it was perfection and this was the opinion of someone who had bedded all types of Fae creatures in his lifetime. His Dragon was heavily muscled, his arms corded, his thighs thick. His chest was a wall of flesh that he wanted to bite. Vulwin's eyes danced over all that tanned, hairless flesh until they settled between his legs.

"Perfect," he breathed again. Iffear's hard cock

glistened with precum as it pressed against his stomach. It was thick and a little darker than his skin, a green tint to it making it as unique as did the slight scale patterns pressed into the delicate flesh. He was rather thick and Vulwin couldn't wait for his turn to take a ride on such an impressive piece.

He had no balls, as Dragons had no need for exterior reproductive organs but the space where they met was taken up by the swollen pink lips of his vagina. As he watched, Iffear began to stroke his cock hard and fast while his other hand dipped down to tease at his labia.

"Fuck me," Iffear demanded now, a growl in his voice, and Vulwin inhaled deeply of his heat scent. He smelled fertile and lush, and his mouth watered at the thought of tasting him in his most intimate of places.

He was on his knees between Iffear's spread legs even before his mate could make another demand of him. He ran his hands over the smooth flesh of his legs as he spread them further. "I can't wait to taste you."

Then he was dipping low, tossing his hair aside as he got his first taste of Dragon flesh.

"Fuck!" Iffear's thighs tightened around his head as Vulwin's tongue teased at his vagina. It wasn't like a human's or a Fae's, exactly; there was no clitoris and his labia was thinner, but it acted much in the same way. His face was dripping with the slick that poured forth from the tasty orifice and Vulwin found himself grunting in pleasure as he buried his face between his lover's thighs.

"Vulwin!" Iffear was arching his hips and fucking into his face, his ass bouncing on the furs as he let himself go. Vulwin understood that his heat was making him a bit more uninhibited than he normally would be, but by his Dragon's own admission, it wasn't much more. Clearly Iffear knew what he wanted. Vulwin lifted up enough so that his tongue trailed over slick pink flesh as his hands cupped his Dragon's hips. He looked up and saw those bright red eyes peering back at him. "Yes, eat me," his lover panted, his hand stroking his cock roughly.

Happy to oblige, Vulwin dipped low again and sank his tongue in deep, his fingers digging into the supple flesh of his ass, holding him steady. Iffear whimpered, his body tingling as he began to trill in a low, hungry tone.

Fuck, it was beautiful. Vulwin moved one hand to stroke his own cock, feeling the need to alleviate some pressure before he embarrassed himself by going off like a geyser for a second time without ever fucking his mate.

"In me, please," Iffear begged, his hips rolling again the tenacious hold he had on them and Vulwin finally gave in to what his mate wanted.

"Gonna ride you hard, my Dragon. Going to claim you like you need."

He pushed up to line his swollen cock against his lover's dripping opening.

"Yes, yes, yes," Iffear chanted, his legs rising up to snap around Vulwin's waist as he began to slide inside.

"Iffear!" Vulwin gasped his Dragon's name as he sank his cock into the slickest, tightest, hottest flesh he had ever been in. "Fuck!

He stopped moving and closed his eyes, struggling to regain some control. His whole body felt struck by lightning as he slowly sank into his mate. His breathing was ragged and his whole body was shaking. He had forgotten this feeling, this hunger to thrust deeply inside, to take, to place his claim. He loomed over his mate, his hands above his shoulders, holding him fast as Iffear began to grind up against him.

"Move!" he demanded, his hand moving rapidly over his cock, tears streaming down his face.

Holding him in place, Vulwin pulled back, growling at the loss of the slick heat surrounding his cock before he thrust back in hard.

Iffear grunted, his legs tightening around his waist so much he could barely move, but Vulwin persevered. He pulled back and slammed deep into his mate's slick heat once more.

"Fuck," he breathed as fire flowed from his belly and sent its heat snaking through all parts of his body. He felt it in his spine, in his chest; his fucking ears were wiggling and burning... Fuck, this was good.

How long had it been since he could actually fuck someone? Getting his rocks off with anal was fun and it satisfied a need, but there was nothing like giving in to the urge to pound a hungry lover into the mattress with a thick hard dick. He was reveling in the fact that he would finally plow someone as much as he was getting off on the fact that his mate beneath him loved what he was doing.

Iffear's hands left his cock and were now digging into the skin of his shoulders, drawing blood and sending sharp bolts of pain through him that only made the pleasure all the sweeter. Growling, he dropped his face into his lover's neck, licking and sucking at the skin there, finding where he was most tender and vulnerable.

Iffear's hands went to his head, fisting his hair and he urged him closer. "Yes," he moaned in abandon. "Harder! Faster. More!"

With a snarl, Vulwin redoubled his efforts in

fucking his mate through the mattress. He shifted Iffear's weight, nearly bending the Dragon in two as he pulled his legs from around his waist and threw them over his shoulders.

His Dragon let out a shrill sound that drove him on, slamming into his body harder, faster, until the only sounds were of his mate's cries and the sound of their wet skin slapping together.

Vulwin felt his cock swell further, growing in a delicious way he now remembered, for it had been so long since he felt this. His mate was wet and tight, his slick dribbling down to cover his balls as he ground in deep, making his Dragon gasp his name.

Oh yes, he remembered how to do this. He gripped Iffear's hands, pulling them over his head, leaving his mate open and vulnerable and he snarled down at him.

"Mine!" he snapped and his Dragon squealed as he drove in deeper than he had before. "Mine!"

His Dragon didn't argue; instead, he turned his head to the side, exposing more of his delicious neck and Vulwin dove in. Before he could stop himself, he let his teeth elongate into fangs and was slamming them into his mate's neck, piercing the skin and drawing his sweet blood as Iffear jerked against him sharply, accepting his dominance even as he rode his cock like he owned it.

"Vulwin!" Iffear was growling, smoke pouring from his nose as his body began to stiffen.

Vulwin didn't know how long he could keep up this demanding pace, but one look at his mate's face, at how his fears relaxed as his body was opening up, was enough to drive him on. He shifted his hips, changing the angle, slamming in deep and curling his hips as his Dragon threw his head back and screamed.

The feel of his inner muscles grasping his cock stole Vulwin's breath. His mate was screaming as his body went mad beneath him. His Dragon was rocking as his cock swelled between their bellies. He pressed down, making sure Iffear's cock was stroked with his stomach with every thrust and his Dragon stiffened in his arms.

Vulwin pulled back, licking at the bite he knew would scar, before he reared back and grabbed his mate by the waist. Then Iffear was coming, crystalline seed exploding from his cock as his walls began to milk his mate.

"By the Five," Vulwin gasped, tears flooding his own eyes as the pressure in his spine broke. With his mate's internal contractions getting harder, Vulwin felt this own release wash over him.

Sobbing in an orgasm that was almost painful, Vulwin bent over his mate, causing him to thrust his body as his hips worked uncontrollably. He knew nothing but the tight hot pleasure of being deep inside his Dragon and releasing his seed as far inside of him as he could get.

His balls ached, his back arched, and his body was racked in spasms as his pleasure overtook him.

He felt his magic flare, silver and black, as it surrounded his mate, covering him, claiming him as his own.

Abruptly the energy that held him suspended broke and he dropped to his Dragon's chest. He felt Iffear's legs fall from around his shoulders to gently frame his body as his Dragon murmured in approval.

"Beautiful," he purred as his Dragon trilled softly underneath him.

He rolled them to the side, whining as his sore cock slipped from his mate's hot body, but he couldn't stop peppering his head and face with small kisses. "You'll be the death of me."

He managed to gasp the words, closing his eyes and letting exhaustion pull him into slumber.

"Not until you do it again," his Dragon purred against the skin of his neck, those sharp teeth grazing his skin. "And again... at least three more times before we rest and do it all over again."

Yes, his Dragon was going to kill him, but what a way to go.

Chapter Five

"What? Three orgasms in a row isn't enough?" Vulwin gave a sharp slap to Iffear's ass as his Dragon purred beneath him.

He slid his sore cock out of Iffear's grasping hole and did his best not to topple over onto the poor Dragon. He looked down at his mate's leaking rosebud and thought it was one most beautiful, nasty things he had ever seen, had ever done. His seed was leaking down to coat his balls, his mark of ownership of the powerful creature, and he reached down to massage the exhausted muscles, helping his reddened hole to close as he attempted to sooth away the soreness. Maybe after a rest he would fuck him full of his seed again and lick it out. It wasn't like they used the anus for more than sex anyway and Vulwin decided he wanted to know his mate in each and every way. But for now his Dragon was listing like he was lost in the storm. His poor Dragon was going through a nasty heat.

Poor Dragon indeed. Iffear may have settled down after the fifth fucking but Vulwin knew he was just resting before the heat frenzy took him again.

He collapsed at his mate's side and ran a trembling hand over his tattooed back. The Dragon etched on his skin was exquisite, a beautiful masterpiece of skin and ink. Vulwin was jealous that someone else had given his beautiful mate such exquisite pain and the ink as a souvenir.

"Not bad for a born-again virgin," Iffear purred, a curl of smoke rolling up from his nostrils as he pushed back against Vulwin. "I thought I would have to instruct you more in the actual fucking."

"Only a born-again virgin in spots." Vulwin

chuckled. "And believe me, I got a lot of practice in knowing what to do to please a partner. Experience is a good teacher after all."

"Mmm." Iffear snuggled down into the furs that covered the bed, his warm body relaxing under Vulwin's caresses. "I like your cock ring."

"Chastity device," Vulwin corrected with a grumble. "And the damn thing won't come off. My father has a sick sense of humor."

"You like the look." Iffear opened one red eye to peer up at him. "You know you do."

"Well, it *is* gold," Vulwin said with a laugh. "I want to drape you in gold."

"Onyx." Iffear mustered up the energy to turn onto his back, exposing a stomach corded with muscle and coated in his own scant release. He was in heat; his body had no need to produce the copious amounts of seed that Vulwin seemed to be pumping out. "I want onyx, mate. I look good in black and I have enough gold."

That said, he took Vulwin's arm and dropped it over his stomach, heedless of his spend, staring down as if comparing their skin colors. "You would think that black, silver, and gold would clash, but on you..." he looked up into Vulwin's eyes. "On you, they are beautiful."

"That's the heat talking." Vulwin ran his hand over his mate's shaved scalp, tugging at his gently rounded ears. "When this heat is done you will start questioning your life decisions."

"When this heat is done I will no doubt still think your natural form is beautiful and my only regret is that I can't get seeded this cycle. I think a child with our coloring would be glorious."

"You can't?" Vulwin had his head propped on

one arm, caressing his mate, but now he sat up, his head tilted to the side. "You feel fertile to me."

"Your ring." Iffear reached down and ran his fingers over the filigree chastity device wrapped snugly around the base of his soft cock. "It's a contraceptive. I can feel the spell holding back any viable seed."

For a moment Vulwin's duel-colored eyes flared in anger before he took a deep breath and settled himself. "This had to be Kno's doing as my father would not concern himself with our sexual habits."

"Maybe your sire wants us to get used to living as an interracial couple before the babies start coming." Iffear shrugged. "Doesn't matter to me. I wasn't prepared for rugrats. One of the reasons I was going to sleep this heat away is because I am no way yet prepared to be a mother."

Vulwin narrowed his eyes at his mate. "For a Dragon, you know a lot of modern human terminology."

"That I do."

"And you understand each and every idiom."

Those red eyes looked amused. "Of course I do."

"How?" He really wanted to know. He was discovering that he was starting to like his mate. He was funny and sarcastic and demanding and might be in heat but was no pushover. Those were characteristics he liked. Also, his body held quite a few scars, reminders of his hard work and badges of his honor in battle. That trick with the Dragon Stone was beyond underhanded and dishonorable. It was cruel and more worthy of humankind than Fae. "I know you said you have been there for over a thousand years, but I assumed you spent most of your time in hiding. Even if you own a tattoo shop, I thought that it was a more recent endeavor."

"You think you are the only earth Fae to make his way in the human world and stay openly?"

Vulwin didn't even hesitate. "Yes."

"Are you that arrogant?" Iffear lifted an onyx eyebrow and Vulwin snorted at him. It was a very human thing to do to show his disdain for the comment, but his mate was sure to understand the context if he was as well versed in humanity as he was claiming.

"Other Fae come and visit, they hide for a time, or they come to make sport with the humans. I have never heard of one making a living out amongst them. I have been there for years and I have never crossed paths with another permanent squatter."

"Well, most Fae discount Dragons."

"I adore Dragons." Vulwin punctuated his statement by dropping his hand low and gripping his mate's cock. Iffear hissed, his back arching up as a low whine rolled from his throat. Vulwin licked his lips as his Dragon's whole body shivered. He looked down at his own swelling cock adorned in chains of gold and decided that he really wasn't that sore.

"You know more about us than most, but we have been out amongst humans for centuries. When places change and people age, we just move."

"So there is a whole Dragon society on the surface that we know nothing about?"

"I wouldn't call it a whole society..." Iffear hissed as his head began to roll from side to side on the furs. "Yes, a little tighter, my mate." He thrust up into Vulwin's grip and the Dhrow happily obliged.

"But there are more than a few of you." Vulwin continued his line of questioning even as he teased his lover, stroking the soft skin of his cock, his fingers dipping low to caress the folds of his cunt. How he loved having several holes to choose from when pleasuring his mate. "And you are but one?"

"Tattoo parlor." Iffear hissed, spreading his legs wider and reaching for Vulwin. "In Baltimore. That place is too weird for anyone to notice anything. There aren't any other Dragons that I've noticed, but there are Pixies and Sprites, and Gargoyles and..." He broke off as Vulwin began to bite at the claiming marks on his neck. "You need to stay with me there. I can show you the world condensed in such a small place."

"I live in New York. Your town wouldn't shock me."

"You live in a town where magic no longer exists only because no one really cares. It has all become background noise. It is too focused in on the mundane task of living. Baltimore is different."

"You really want me there that bad?"

In an instant Iffear had him spun around and lying on his stomach. Oh yeah, this was good.

"I want you that bad," Iffear whispered in his ear, nipping at the top before licking the pain away.

"Oh... unngh... yeah," Vulwin moaned, pushing his ass back into his mate's touch. "It's been too long."

"Well, my heat is basically over," Iffear snarled in his ear before he shoved Vulwin's hair to the side and exposed his neck. "Now I think it's my turn."

Vulwin tried not to wail his pleasure as his mate slapped his ass cheeks lightly and purred at the bounce it produced.

"Nice ass. I didn't think swordsmen developed so much in the posterior."

"Archer," Vulwin hissed as his ass was slapped again. "I'm an archer."

"Climbing trees and running, huh?" his mate

purred before delivering several more slaps to his flesh. Vulwin could feel the heat build as his Dragon warmed his ass. It only made him harder. "Such pretty skin."

"I am speckled," Vulwin hissed, craning his neck to look over his shoulder at his grinning mate.

"Your skin is like the night's sky, Vulwin, kissed by stars. I love flying in the night."

Iffear hovered over him, the weight of his body pushing him into the furs. The feel of his Dragon hovering above him was delicious. All that power contained in a small tight package that was all for him. He moaned, arching his ass backwards, sighing as he felt his Dragon's hard cock settle in the cleft of his ass.

"Fly me," Vulwin invited. "It's been too long since I've been filled."

"Greedy."

"You had your fun." Vulwin wiggled his ass and dropped his head, letting his hair cover his face so he could peer at his lover through the silvery mass. "My turn."

Iffear scoffed then blew an almost scalding hot breath down his spine. "By the Five," Vulwin hissed, writhing on the furs beneath them. Heat was such a turn-on for him... His lover was unnaturally hot, and wrapping himself around him was like wrapping himself around liquid sex. Now all of that restored passion was on top of him, teasing him, and he was going to go mad if his lover didn't give it to him.

"Greedy," Iffear murmured again before Vulwin felt the wet heat of his tongue trailing down his back. He hissed as his lover ignited fires throughout his body. His ass popped up and his hands fisted the furs, a whimper falling from his throat.

Damn right he was greedy. He had spent too

many years being an exclusive bottom for his ass not to
get greedy for a good hard dicking. And his mate had
such a nice, scaled cock. He couldn't wait to feel it
splitting him open.

By now Iffear was leaving nips and bites down
his back until he reached the rise of his plump ass.
"You taste like earth, Dhrow," Iffear purred.

"Is that a good thing?" he asked, trying not to
pant. His mate's breath was wafting over his cleft and
he wanted to reach back, spread himself open, and
demand attention.

"A very good thing," Iffear answered as his
fingers danced along the crack of his ass, teasing him.

"Wanna know where I taste better?" he said,
tossing his hair back and turning enough to stare Iffear
down.

His Dragon smirked at him before his large
hands were on his cheeks, spreading him wide open.

Groaning, Vulwin dropped his forehead to the
furs and tried to hold on. His mate had no shame, just
like him. He loved it.

"Oh, your tiny little hole is silver!" Iffear ran a
few fingers over his opening, pressing softly and
making Vulwin burn with want and the promise of
penetration. "It's so cute."

"Why don't you give it a kiss," he smarted back
then laughed as his Dragon laid a hard slap to his ass.

"Why don't I just pound on this ass instead?"

"I have something for you to mount…"

Then his words were lost as he felt his mate's
very slick, very hot, very long tongue dance over his
opening.

"Fuck," he shouted, fisting the furs as his lover
spread his cheeks wide and began to lap down his cleft
then gently over his hole.

It was a hot, slow feeling that made his bones melt. Fuck, he had not had this in his real form in so long, and it looked as if his lover really liked pleasing him this way. He felt himself being spread wider and Iffear hummed under his breath as he licked him deeper, relaxing his hole until he felt one thick finger slip inside.

"Yes!" he moaned, squeezing his eyes shut as lightning began to explode in his brain. Then he was pushing back, riding his lover's face as his whole body began to quiver.

When Iffear slipped his tongue deep inside, he gave up all pretense of control. His cock was hard, pressed between his stomach and the furs, his balls were heavy and tingling as lust spread through his body. He rocked back and forth, loving the slick slide of his mate's tongue, but it wasn't enough.

"Come on, fuck me!" he demanded, and his Dragon chucked.

"Demanding little bottom --"

"I learned it from fucking you," he shouted. "Now return the favor."

"I need to prep you --"

"Dhrow!" he shouted back. "Hungry, horny Dhrow. Fuck me now."

He finally reached back and grabbed his own cheeks, spreading them wide as his Dragon added another finger. He wailed, "Iffear!"

"But I love dipping my fingers into you," he insisted, and Vulwin began to curse loudly in three human languages and two Fae.

He was so horny his stomach was burning. His body was tense, he was aching in ways he didn't think was possible, and even more, he craved the intimacy he had grown used to sharing with his mate. He wanted to experience all of Iffear, but his mate was a fate-damned tease.

"I swear, I will end you --"

He cut off as his mate gripped him by the hips and flipped him once more. He leaned back, his legs splayed wide, his hair in his face.

"I want to see you," Iffear murmured and Vulwin nearly choked at the picture his Dragon presented.

His mate was thick and muscular, his eyes blazing red while a smile curled his lips and a small cloud of smoke rolled up from his nostrils. One large hand was stroking his thick cock, spreading drops of crystalline pre-cum over the spade-shaped head, the other teasing at his wet cunt. He hovered over him, a being of infinite power and wild magic, and Vulwin had never felt so small or so lucky.

His mate grabbed his thighs, spreading them wide around his body as he bent over him. He paused in stroking his cock to brush the long river of hair from Vulwin's face.

Vulwin knew his eyes were glittering; he could feel the power growing in him as he gazed at his mate. He bit his lip as he placed both feet flat on the furs, opening himself for his Dragon.

Iffear didn't waste any time accepting the invite. He dropped over him, both hands beside his head as he allowed his long tongue to drop forth and lap at his nipples.

"Fates!" Vulwin wailed as that long, divertingly delicious tongue traveled over his chest and then dipped down to wrap around his cock. Iffear lowered his head, pulling his lover's cock deep into the hot cavern of his mouth and Vulwin instantly lost control and started fucking his face.

Iffear must have loved his mate doing this, because he opened his throat and swallowed him deep.

Vulwin close his eyes and whined, the feeling of his mate's throat... so tight, so hot and perfect. His hands left the furs and gripped his own hair instead. Everything was tingling; his skin was on fire. He was slowly losing his mind. He started as he felt his lover's finger slide into his hole.

"Wet," his Dragon murmured, pulling back and licking his lips as if Vulwin tasted like the most succulent candy. "I like this."

"Fuck me," Vulwin insisted, caught between the extreme pleasure of having his mate's thick fingers split his hole open and the mind-blowing ecstasy of having his mate swallow him to the root, his tongue teasing at the gold ring at the base of his cock. He was suddenly a Fae with an embarrassment of riches and he was enjoying every damn one of them.

The hunger in his ass grew and he felt his balls drawing up in preparation to explode so he grabbed his Dragon's shoulders, pulling him back. "I want to go with you inside me."

"I can arrange that."

That was all that needed to be said. Vulwin reached down and grabbed his lover's cock, caressing the swollen spade-shaped head.

He whimpered, honestly thinking he would shed a tear as he caressed Iffear's marvelous cock. The scales were harder under the soft skin, and he couldn't wait to feel them along his walls. Iffear was thick, so thick he could barely get his hands around him, and it made his hole twitch. Quickly he began to stroke his Dragon, rubbing the slick he produced over the head and wetting him up proper. With a sly grin he ran his fingers over his mate's pussy and collected the slick there too, laughing as his Dragon hissed and threw his head back in pleasure at the intimate touch.

Vulwin nearly screamed as he felt his mate's teeth on his nipples, nibbling gently before he began marking this chest with bites and sucks. He was going to fucking die before this was all done.

"Now," he demanded, pulling at his mate's hips and finally, Iffear pushed his thighs up further, situating himself between his legs before pressing the wide head of his cock against his hole.

When his lover hesitated, Vulwin screamed, "I'm to going to break you, you fucking Dragon! Fuck me *now*!"

After hearing that, Iffear's eyes narrowed and then his Dragon was slamming into him hard.

"Yes!" he wailed, throwing his head back as his hands clawed at Iffear's chest. *This!* This is what he wanted. The feeling of a rock-hard cock splitting him in two. And his scale marks… they were dragging at his walls, igniting nerve endings that had tears running from his eyes and his mouth babbling nonsense.

Fuck, this was perfect. His Dragon was hot and hard and hitting him in all the right ways. Out of his control, his legs wrapped around Iffear's waist, his feet digging into his ass to get him in closer. And his Dragon hummed deeply, his whole body vibrating as he ground his hips in small circles.

"Oh Fates," Vulwin screamed, his body alight with ecstasy as his mate took him deep. His body began to tremble, his stomach tightened, and the wildest noises he had ever made rolled from his throat.

Then Iffear slowly pulled out to slam back in and Vulwin lost his damn mind.

He was aware of nothing, just his Dragon's push and pull inside his body. He was cocooned in heat, overwhelmed by magic, lost in a pleasure he never thought was possible.

His mate was taking him to heights he had never reached before. He was coming undone.

He whimpered his lover's name, pulling him down into a kiss that Iffear immediately took control over. His long tongue slid around his mouth, tasting him. Vulwin sucked on that slick appendage and moaned as his lover's long tongue began to taste the back of his throat. Soon Iffear was fucking his mouth like he was fucking his body and Vulwin was losing it.

One hand pulled away from where it was tearing at Iffear's back to reach for his own hard, needy cock.

"Yeah," Iffear pulled back to purr. "Stroke yourself off. I want to see it."

It was a damn good idea so Vulwin fisted his leaking cock, tightening his hold on its cowl. He began curling up into his fist and pumping back onto that heavenly thickness that was his mate's cock. Faster and faster he moved, losing his mind and becoming lost in waves of sensation that had him crying out and begging for more.

In the midst of this, he felt his lover drop his head to his neck and instinctively, Vulwin tilted his head to the side, exposing his vulnerable flesh to his Dragon.

Faster and faster he was being pounded and his nerves were screaming for release. His thighs were burning, his heart was racing, and he need just a little more… just a little…

His mate's teeth pierced his neck, marking him, and in a violent flash of green and black magic, he pushed back and screamed. His balls slammed against the base of his cock and his orgasm tore through him with the force of a raging storm.

He wailed again as his mate redoubled his efforts and then with a shout, he ripped his teeth from his neck and Vulwin felt his body filled with the scalding-hot seed of his mate.

Abruptly they collapsed together onto the furs, Iffear lapping at his neck, closing the wounds and ensuring that the bite mark, their mark of bonding, would be there for all to see.

"So we return to Baltimore," Vulwin groaned, wiping the tears from his eyes before he settled his hands back on Iffear's waist, his hips still jerking up as he rode out the last of his climax. "You make a compelling argument."

"You can model from anywhere," Iffear mumbled into his neck, his tongue lapping at the beads of sweat that glistened there before his fingers moved down his chest to pluck at a still sensitive nipple. "You can fly to where you need to go. They have an international airport."

"Too true," Vulwin agreed as he felt his eyes begin to close.

They needed to clean up a bit and solidify their plans to move as soon as possible. He was already tired of politics and his father's machinations... but first a well-deserved nap, snuggling against the warm, hard body of his Dragon.

Dragon Alliance (Dragon 2)
A Paranormal Women's Fiction Novella
Stephanie Burke

Iffear comes to Vulwin at his most vulnerable, but as their magical enemies and a plot to destroy the Dhrovish throne make themselves known, the newly mated couple find themselves drawing closer together in order to survive.

Chapter One

"So, this is nice." In his human skin, Vulwin, aka Win Arcarius, was an unmistakable albino black man with long, pale blond hair and bi-colored eyes that were to die for -- or at least that was what his agent believed. He looked around his new quarters and gave them an approving smile.

He was tall, sleekly muscled with large eyes, one green eye and one silver, that peered out at audiences from a set of lashes so long they looked like they had to be fake. His cheekbones were high, his lips were full, his skin was an extremely pale tan, and his attitude, like his clothing, was fierce.

Beside him walked his proud mate, his dragon, who was wearing a tight, white tank top, a pair of tight denim jeans, and the most kick-ass pair of black riding boots that the world had ever seen. Probably because they were Dhrow-made and designed with his protection in mind.

In comparison, Win looked ready for the runway in his long, flowing red tunic and loose black pants. He was wearing black leather sandals on his feet and was resplendent in his gold jewelry... huge bangles on his wrists, several delicate chains in his ears, and rings on every finger and toe. He was a model in every sense of the word, and walking into this upscale tattoo shop and piercing parlor was guaranteed to bring traffic to a halt.

Strutting before them was a tiny black cat, Chinsie, who looked more of the human kind of pet than anything she looked like Under the Hill. Around her neck was a spiked collar of gold, and she moved with the same protective attitude she had presented before. She was a bad-ass and she knew it.

Once inside the small brownstone mansion, Chinsie took off like a shot to a bay window covered in plush silence pillows, obviously her spot in the shop front room, and perched herself like royalty.

"I thought you said you'd be gone for a month, bossman," the short woman behind a tall glass counter said as she put down a sketch pad, looked up, and -- "Well I'll be damned." Her mouth dropped open when Iffear reached out and grabbed Win's hand.

"Plans change," he offered, his voice deep and gravelly and still enough to put a shiver in Win's loins. Was there ever a case of a creature passing on being in heat to another creature of a different species? He still didn't know, but damn, he was feeling like he was in rut around his mate. "This is --"

"Win Arcarius," the woman managed, eyes growing wide in shock. "Supermodel and spokesman for about a bazillion products. I'm sure you know you're beautiful, but do you know how beautiful you are?" While she spoke, she not so secretly pulled her phone off the counter and began taking shots of them.

The smile that spread across Win's lips was genuine as he pulled Iffear in closer. "Thank you." His voice was accented in a way that most humans could not place, though the companies he represented loved it. "It's nice of you to say so."

At their close contact, the woman's smile became a smirk. "Vacation, boss? Going to Europe for a month or so? So is that what the kids are calling it these days?"

"Mai," Iffear groaned and Win smirked back at her. "What happened is none of your business."

"Mai." Win grinned. "I think I like your style."

"Mai Wind," she introduced herself, her purple-tipped afro adding height to her short stature.

"Resident piercer and apprentice tattooist. And you better like my style. I'm wearing your name on my ass." She hopped off her high stool and walked around to meet them, spinning around at the last minute to show the stylized *WA* on the back pocket of her pants. She turned to face them, holding out her hand as she drew closer. "And dare I pray you want to get your tongue pierced today? A nipple?" She pointed to his crotch. "Something in the lower region, perhaps?"

"I can't take the time off from using my tongue to let it heal." Win almost sounded disappointed as he shook her hand. "And if I can't take the time to let my tongue heal, then anything lower is out of the question."

"Ohh, kinky." Mai chuckled before looking up at Iffear. "I hope he's pulled you from your life of celibacy and popped your second virginity so you can stop being such a raging bitch."

Win's laughter was loud and obnoxious and he didn't care. Talk about getting your roles reversed.

"Why do I like you?" Iffear snarked down at her, tapping her on the nose with his free hand. "And why haven't I fired you yet?"

"Because I am the one who keeps your sorry ass organized. What would you do without me, boss?" She laughed, punching him lightly on the arm. "Like the time those drunk twin sorority girls --"

"So," he spoke loudly over her, "This is my shop manager and main piercer, Mai Wind. She's snarky."

"I like snark." Win chuckled.

"And Mai, this is Win Arcarius, my husband."

As he dropped this bombshell, Mai's mouth dropped open again in shock as she struggled to find a word to say.

Win, of course, found this hysterical and began

to laugh out loud as he leaned against his mate.

"Husband... Did you sign a prenup?" She turned serious eyes to Iffear. "Because you're gonna want to sign a prenup."

Win's laughter, at this point, was so hard that he began to choke as tears ran down his face. "Prenup!" he wailed while Iffear eyed his manager with disdain.

"He's worth more than me," Iffear pointed out.

"Oh." She nodded, turning to stare at Win again. "Did *you* sign a prenup?"

"We'll be going now," Iffear interrupted her before she could say anything else. "I have to show Win our living area."

"Is that code for screw?" Mai called back as Iffear hustled to the back of the shop and the hidden elevator that would take them to the living quarters. "Because that sounds like code for hot, sweaty screwing. And can I sell that photo? I haven't heard any buzz about the modeling world's bad-boy getting hitched!"

"No!" Iffear called out as Win shouted, "I don't care, but if you sell it to a tabloid, I get half!"

"Fucking awesome!"

"You know you just gave her permission to start a media frenzy, right?" Iffear grumbled at Win as he pressed his thumbprint to a panel of the hidden elevator. "And knowing Mai, she's gonna do it."

"What's a little media coverage between friends?" Win nearly choked on his laughter.

"Friends? You don't even know her." When the elevator doors opened, his mate hustled him inside, rolling his eyes at him and the attempt he made to slow down their progress to start more mischief.

"But I already know she and I are going to be good friends. I'm going to need something to do while you're poking holes in people."

"I got something you can poke a hole into," Iffear purred, burying his face in his mate's neck and inhaling his scent before bending to lap at the tender skin.

"Ah, still in heat, are we?"

"Yes, we are." Iffear pressed him against the nearest wall and began to lap at the delicate skin of his neck. "Stop hiding from me."

"If my mate insists," Vulwin purred and let his glamour slowly bleed away.

* * *

Iffear stepped back and watched the way the pale color of his mate's skin began to slowly bleed into the star-speckled black. He was starting to love that skin and the transformation.

It started in his face, the paleness crumpling, tearing, and falling away like aged tissue paper. Intrigued, he reached out his left hand, extending the claws he normally concealed and ripped through the delicate material, exposing his lover's chest to his hungry gaze.

For his part, Vulwin relaxed against the wall, licking his lips slowly, leaving behind a silvery sheen on the nearly black lips as his hair shimmered from a pale blond to a startling silver.

Watching the slow transformation of his mate's body was better than watching porn. Seeing the human guise disintegrate and fall away from Vulwin's beautiful body was enough to make Iffear's hard cock throb in his jeans and his hearts start pounding his chest. He inhaled deeply, and the scent of human glamour faded away until he could smell that dark spiciness that was all Dhrow.

"You going to just stand there and watch?" Vulwin asked, his eyes glowing as they ran over

Iffear's own body. "Or are you going to participate, mate-of-mine?"

"Just enjoying the show," Iffear murmured as he gave in to the need to touch. He ran his fingers over Vulwin's face, caressing the soft skin there, taking in the eyes too large to be human, the cheekbones sharp enough to cut glass, the full, dangerous lips that could suckle him into submission or spout words that could tear an enemy to shreds.

And all that was his.

The thought made him purr deeply in his chest as white smoke poured from his nose, creating a smoky atmosphere, a world where only he and his mate existed.

"You know, you are allowed to touch." Vulwin reached out and very slowly ran one finger down his chest, pressing into the cotton of his shirt. Iffear's purr grew louder as the shirt parted at his touch, and continued melting until it disappeared from his body completely. Fuck, his mate's power was such a turn-on. "I intend to touch a lot."

Iffear's pants grew wet with his arousal and the need to be penetrated was being eclipsed by the need to penetrate. He wanted... needed to fuck his mate into submission, to make himself one with the power his mate so easily yielded, and ride out the storm they would create together.

With a growl, he reached out and wrapped his arms around Vulwin's hips, and instantly the cheeky Dhrow leaped up and wrapped both legs around Iffear's waist, his heavy cock pulsing against Win's stomach through the thin material of his pants. The strength in those thighs was stunning, and Iffear couldn't wait to pound him through a mattress with those thighs pulling him closer, demanding more.

Vulwin was a prince, determined to get his way, assured that he was correct in all things. It was time to show him that he couldn't control everything. Iffear slid his hands down to his mate's plump ass, squeezing the flesh as he turned and strode through his halls to his bedroom, the tall bundle of Dhrovish flesh in his arms giggling like a maniac as Iffear threw him onto the bed.

"About damn time," Vulwin teased as he shimmied out of his pants and kicked them aside, lying back naked, exposed, and unashamed. He ran one dark hand over his chest, plucking at his dark nipples before trailing his fingers over his corded stomach. He gripped his cock hard, toying at the ring at the base for a moment before his fingers slid down to the heart-shaped head, his fingers toying with the slit there. "For a dragon in heat, you are incredibly slow when it comes to taking what you want. So… are we going to fuck, my mate? Are you going to crawl across this bed and sit on what I am so generously offering to you?" He stroked his hard cock once more and leered at Iffear as he did so, the silvery precum sliding down his shaft making his stroking more fluid.

Vulwin threw back his head and hissed, his eyes small slits that stared at Iffear with liquid lust and intent. It was the look of a male who knew what he wanted and was used to getting it.

Offering him a lazy smile in return, Iffear unfastened his jeans. Instead of pulling them down, he slid his hands into the front to gently caress his own swollen dick, closing his eyes for a moment as his empty hole clenched down while his hunger grew. He wanted to be filled, but he wanted to be inside his hot prince even more. Some of his instincts would have to wait. He was getting a piece of that ass. He wanted to sink himself so deep into his mate that he would imprint himself on his heart. He wanted there to be no doubt that the silver prince Vulwin Valas was owned body and soul by a dragon.

A wave of his own hand sent his jeans exploding into a smoky black puff of air, and he stood before his mate, proud and naked. Silvery streams of slick trailed, thick and warm, down his thighs, as his dick ached, so hard it pressed against his stomach. He could feel the outlines of his scales pressing through his human skin as parts of his own guise of humanity began to slide away. His tongue flashed out, tasting the air around his mate, pulling in the flavor of lust and heat and Dhrow.

Vulwin, for his part, was sitting up and taking notice, his hand still stroking his dick while the other came up to tease and pull at his nipples. His Dhrow was nearly panting as the dragon moved closer.

There was no furniture in Iffear's bedroom, save for a wall-length mirror that hid his closet and a bed. The bright light of the day from the skylight over the bed settled around his mate like a mantle, making the constellations of silvery dots on Vulwin's skin glisten as he dropped his cock and reached out for his lover. But Iffear had other ideas.

He reached out and gripped Vulwin's offered hand, but with a jerk yanked his Vulwin from the bed, pulling the taller Dhrow against his chest. He hissed as their hard cocks rubbed each other, and for a moment he wanted to give into his instincts and drop to his knees before his mate, his legs spread, his ass presented to be taken and filled, to be used as nothing more than a receptacle for his mate's seed until his belly was filled with a baby. But he pushed those feelings aside as he spun around. In two steps his mate was pressed into the mirror, his face turned to the side to stare at Iffear. Vulwin began to pant, the scent of his arousal growing deeper and stronger.

"I want to touch," Iffear purred into his ear, grinding his hard dick into the trench of Vulwin's perfect ass, "The way I want."

He continued. "I'm going to take you, Vulwin. I am going to wreck this pretty little ass of yours, fill you so good that you'll crave my touch and pant after my dick like you're the one in heat."

Vulwin shuddered, with a low growl rolling from his chest as he pressed back into Iffear's thrusts, his mouth going slack.

Iffear fisted a hand into the glorious silk of his hair and jerked his head back, taking his mouth, invading it with his tongue. He savored the flavors of his mate, drawing in that Dhrow spice as his tongue danced along the sharp teeth and ran along the roof of his mouth. His mate tasted like magic, and he exhaled a puff of smoke into Win's mouth, feeling his own magic invade his mate's body.

He stepped back and gripped Vulwin's waist, pulling him far enough from the mirror and bending him over so that his cock hung low and his balls swung free.

Bent over, his mate was a fever dream of lust as those hard muscles flexed beneath the black-speckled skin. His long hair hung forward and hid his face while plump, rounded ass cheeks flexed. He ran his hands over the hard expanse of flesh that was his, and exhaled more smoke as he bit back a roar. He had to have his mate, had to stake his claim and mark him as owned by a dragon.

He dropped to his knees and palmed the rounded cheeks of his Vulwin's ass before spreading him open to his gaze.

Vulwin whimpered at the action, his knees shaking before he stiffened them and secured his balance. Iffear looked up in time to see Vulwin looking over his shoulder, his head twisting farther than any human could ever dream of doing. "You gonna eat me out?"

Iffear's response was automatic. "Like you were my last meal." His thumbs caressed the dark opening to his mate's body, noting that he was lubricating as if he was in heat as well. Another Dhrow fact he tucked away into his mental file as Iffear inhaled deeply. The spicy smell was strong, ethereal, so delicious it made his mouth water. He leaned forward and let his tongue caress Vulwin's opening.

At the first slick touch of his tongue, Vulwin's head snapped forward and he began to curse in at least three Fae languages.

Iffear closed his eyes and began to lap at the small opening while one hand lifted to caress Vulwin's vibrating cock. His mate was so hot to the touch, a delight for his senses, Iffear decided, as he gave the hard dick a stroke, before dropping it to palm his heavy balls.

He slid his tongue in deeper and moaned at the taste of his mate while Vulwin began to pant his name.

Vulwin was trembling, starting to sweat as Iffear teased his silken walls with gentle flicks of his tongue. Iffear could feel his mate's muscles flutter and tremble as he worked him hard with his tongue. He blew a puff of smoke here too, onto his mate, as Vulwin yelled at the heat and the tinge of magic that invaded his body. His fingers scraped at the cold glass of the mirror as his knees threaded to give way. "Fuck, Iffear!" he sobbed and Iffear grinned, knowing that his magic was making Win's body more sensitive, caressing it from the inside as he continued to lap at his delicate flesh, driving his mate hard into this need to be taken.

Iffear could feel his own dick leak and throb in hunger, with the desire to be pressed deep inside the body of his lover. Precum was making a small puddle on the floor between his legs and his own hole flexed hungrily at its empty state. He was leaking from both ends and the taste of his mate on his tongue, the feel of his slick walls, his scent, the sound of him crying in ecstasy, drove him with an almost overriding need to push into his mate's flesh. He wanted to fuck and to be fucked at the same time. He almost gave into his heat and begged for Vulwin to take him, but resolved to follow through with his original plan. His mate would be drenched in his magic, his power, and all who looked at him would know he was possessed by a dragon.

After another moment of torture, he pulled back, giving his mate's hole one final lick before he moved back and surged to his feet.

"I'm going to fuck you, Vulwin," he purred as he slid two fingers into his mate's ass with no difficulty. As a Dhrow, Vulwin required no prep work in order to be fucked, but Iffear wanted to feel his silken walls clenched around his fingers like he had clenched around Iffear's tongue, as he would clench around Iffear's hard dick.

At his words, Vulwin began to purr himself, pushing his ass back, fucking himself desperately on Iffear's fingers.

"Yes, My Dhrow." Iffear bent over his lover's magnificent back end and breathed into his high, pointed ear. "I'm going to fill you full and fuck you raw."

"P-please," Vulwin stammered, his whole body quivering as he pressed desperately back into the fingers spearing him open. "Please, Iffear. Please, my dragon…"

No one in their right mind could resist that invitation. Iffear pulled his fingers out of the slick, grasping heat and pressed the head of his dick to the small opening. He gave one heavy thrust and then roared as he closed his eyes and lost himself in the perfect heat of his mate.

He ground himself in deeply, whining at the slick hard walls that gripped at his cock, pulling him in deeper. He gripped his mate's hips so tightly he was sure the dark skin would be bruised as he rocked his own hips from side to side and listened as his mate screamed out his pleasure.

He had to thrust, to take, to own, so he pulled his hips back and slammed forward. He groaned in satisfaction as his mate screamed his name and eagerly began to fuck himself on the hard length splitting him open wide.

"So fucking perfect," Iffear growled, before gripping his mate's shoulders and slamming into him deeply again and again.

Vulwin whined, slamming himself back, panting as his silver freckles began to glow when Iffear's magic arched up to touch his.

"So fucking perfect," Iffear moaned as he felt his magic rose in answer.

Smoke began to pour from his nose and mouth as he felt his wings explode from his back. With a snarl, he bent over to wrap his arms around his lover's chest and then pulled Vulwin up to face the mirror, hefting him off his feet while flexing his thighs to keep pounding into that delicious ass.

"Look at us!" he roared and watched in the mirror as his mate's eyes began to glow silver as he peered into the mirror.

Win moaned loudly, his head dropping back to rest on Iffear's shoulder as he gave himself into his possession, and his gaze flittered over their heaving bodies. His mate's wings spread out wide, and Win reached up and wrapped his arms around Iffear's neck. He tilted his head to the side, an act of submission, and he cried out to continue.

"Yes, Iffear," he sobbed. "More! Give me more!"

Iffear pushed him back against the mirror, letting Win's toes touch the ground, and he slammed into him repeatedly, growling at the lifting give of Win's flesh, his hole's milking grip.

The room was filled with smoke and the scent and sounds of a primal mating. Iffear arched his back, his wings spreading to their fullest as he fucked his mate and his prince welcomed each touch and caress.

All too soon, he felt his mate stiffen in his arms, and he reached a hand down to grip Win's cock, jerking it to the hard rhythm of his thrusts.

Vulwin threw back his head and screamed as his cock pulsed in his dragon's hands, and he shot his silvery seed against the mirror.

The sight, sound, feel, and the smell of his mate's release had Iffear tipping over as well. He threw back his head and roared as his wings wrapped around them both, as he slammed his cock as deep as he could get into his mate's body and felt his own heated release fill his lover to overflowing. He thrust again and again as his body spasmed while his knees grew weak as he poured all that he was into his prince.

"Yes, yes! Fill me!" Vulwin was moaning, grinding down on his dick as if he was loath to lose even one precious drop.

Iffear tightened his arms around his lover as he dropped to his knees, exhaustion overtaking him. His thighs were wet with his flow of slick, his cock was soaking inside his Dhrow, his limbs felt useless and at the same time his whole body tingled, vibrated with the touch of their combined magic.

He found himself purring as he released his grip on his lover to stroke that silvery-white hair and feel Win's soft skin, suffused with magic, arch under his touch.

"We've got to do that again," Vulwin finally murmured, and Iffear grunted in agreement.

He was content. He could feel their magic blend as he felt the power and strength of this Dhrow who claimed him, freed him, and trusted him.

Smoke rolled from his nose as he made himself and his mate comfortable on the plush carpet as they both drifted off to sleep. He owned his prince just as his prince owned him. He relished the feeling of love and being loved.

Chapter Two

"You just happened to have a shoot at The Harbor?" Iffear adjusted his dark shades as he allowed Win to press him into a tall camp chair set up in front of the camera and lighting rig, but behind all the people operating the equipment.

"I mentioned to my agent that I had gotten married and that I was relocating to Baltimore. It just so happened that Gucci was debuting a nautical line and hosting an invitation-only show here. Things just worked out."

Iffear gave one final look to the backdrop before he turned and offered him a smile. "I've gotta go and take off the war paint --"

"Your skin is perfect. I don't see why they needed to pack all that shit on your face in the first place." His words made his mate smile.

"Well, if it wasn't for this makeup, the lights would make my face flat and pale as hell. The make-up gives me dimension. A camera is no substitute for the human eye and it has to be fooled into seeing what unnatural lights hide."

"And it's a way to pander to the makeup gurus," Iffear added, rolling his eyes as his mate laughed.

"That too. This won't take long."

With one last gentle press of his lips, Vulwin turned toward the trailer they had set up for makeup and costuming for him and the other four models involved in the shoot.

Iffear had watched in amazement as his sarcastic but funny mate became a cold elitist as soon as he stepped on set. All the models were beautiful, but each had something extra that made them stand out from the pretty crowd. Chastity had a sweet, bubbly nature with more than a hint of badassery that showed in each stand or pose she made. Charles was a thick, beautiful black man with perfectly trimmed hair, a well-groomed beard, and enough beautiful ink to make the tattoo artist in him sit up and take notice. He was seduction on two feet. Every move he made exuded sensuality. Wraith was the polar opposite of Charles, snow-white hair, with a muscular build, and icy gray eyes. Whereas Charles was seductive, Wraith was in-your-face sexy and not afraid to show it. Juli was Asian with waist-length hair and stunning brown eyes that peered into your soul. Her complexion was flawless, and she could give you a Lolita look without even trying, then turn around and be a master of sophistication. Win rounded out the group with his cold, imperial attitude and flashes of amusement that showed through when he wanted them to.

The shoot had been fun to watch as the photographers catcalled and made jokes with the crew. Music had blared, a crowd had formed, and the models played it up for the brand and for the people watching. Now Win, by reason of being the last model to take solo shots, was the final model to use the dressing trailer. The others had already changed, and either blended in with the crowd and walked away, or dressed up again and gone to other shoots or destinations.

Iffear sat and waited. He took a few business cards from photographers wanting to shoot him and the ink his arms exposed, and fielded even more questions about his relationship with Win. He ignored the ruder ones and smiled at the curious. If they wanted to know, they would have to wait for Mai to sell those damn photos or for Win to make a statement. Either way he was bored with waiting and ready to go find his mate. At last the trailer door opened, and Win emerged wearing jeans and a stylized dragon T-shirt he had definitely not been wearing to the shoot. In fact, he'd worn sleeping pants and an oversized, long-sleeved Henley there. Iffear offered him an eyebrow and a questioning look.

"It's not like I've seen you in dragon form, so I imagined this is kind of what you looked like," Win pointed out about the shirt, and Iffear had to concede his point.

"I am rather large," he said. "I'd need a lot of space to change and show you."

"You look like your back tattoo?" Win asked curiously as Iffear stood up, and Win reached for his hand.

"Not at all." He laughed when Win shot him a look. "I am not that conceited, lover. I save that for you. I just liked the art."

Win used his free hand to wave at the remaining crew before they began the short walk back to their car. It was tourist season in downtown Baltimore. Cars were parked all along Light Street, and tourists were everywhere, taking pictures of the buildings, ships, and the colorful people who inhabited the city.

The air was warm and the sounds of laughter and life that filled the teeming city filled the air. Iffear tugged a little harder on Win's hand and pulled him closer to his side. Despite the human glamour, he could still see the Dhrow he was mated to. Under the human guise he could see how the larger than human eyes, with their fascinating dual color, glinted in curiosity as he looked around and took everything in. The silver sparkles that painted his skin seemed to glisten brighter in excitement. Vulwin never lost that innate Dhrow curiosity that had stood his people in good stead over the generations.

Dhrow people were the most curious of all the Fae. They were connected to the earth in ways that most Fae could not contemplate. They were of the earth, and as long as there was life in the land they occupied, they could draw power from it. Metals were not a weakness, as silver was for the Goblin-folk or iron for most Fae. The Dhrow harvested and utilized these metals, sang them from the earth to create such beautiful and sophisticated jewelry and pendants.

He thought about the Dragon Stone that had been his possession and how, at his request, Vulwin had sung it back into the earth, setting his long-dead ancestor to rest. It was a beautiful and complicated bit of magic his mate had pulled off, and the Dhrow had managed to do it with no visible loss of energy at all.

His mate. Never in all his years living both Under the Hill and in the human world did he ever think he would bind himself to another. For one thing, dragons were nearly eternal. They were among the longest-lived creatures due to their connection to the earth, and that meant he would be chained to whoever he took to mate for an eternity. Another staggering issue was that unlike most Children of the Five Fates, he enjoyed being around humanity.

Humans were odd creatures, childlike in a lot of ways. They could be violent and bigoted, yet retained the ability to change when the proper motivation was applied. They created such beautiful monuments for life and death, yet seemed to have an insane fear of both. Each generation changed and evolved into something that was completely new and possibly dangerous, and he enjoyed sitting back and watching the tides shift around them.

He never thought he would ever meet another

Fae creature who shared his fascination with humankind. He was content to return to his homeland and ride out each heat asleep and safe in his caves. He knew that a time would come when his instinct would drive him to seek a proper mate, but he always thought he would find another dragon who had the same fascination about the human world and believe what he did interesting enough to stick around and knock him up. He never expected to be drawn from his own home and into the arms of a steamy Elvhen Lord when he was at his weakest.

It was offensive and ignorant to draw him out with the petrified fetus of one of his line. It threw him enough that he could not resist the spells that stunned him long enough for them to chain him with ensorcelled metals and drag him to the Gray Gully as if he was some kind of dangerous sacrifice. It was all he could do to send a summons to his familiar and have Chinsie meet them on the trail. She was good protection for him, and the proof was that all he'd lost was a shirt when an Elvhen guard got too frisky or overcome with Iffear's mating scent. Nearly losing an eye to his vengeful familiar had ended that for the guards. It was a good thing that they were knowledgeable enough about dragons to know that if he or his familiar had been harmed, the racket he would have raised would have brought every dragon nearby roaring for retribution. A war between the Dragon and the Elvhen would only lead to the destruction of their hard-fought peace and most of the Elvhen clans in the area. Dragons were isolationists, but when one was threatened, they could not resist the call to arms. The dragon army hadn't gathered and flown in formation for eons, and most Fae would like it to stay that way. Dragon Fire was a terrible, nearly uncontrollable, thing once loosed. It would scorch the earth black to reach and destroy its intended target, taking out anything and anyone in its path. It was one of the reasons that Dragon-kind stayed neutral in most Fae conflicts unless provoked. Rape or sexual assault would have led to the Elvhen world burning down around them.

Still, the noble who had collected him had had what smelled like generations of dragon blood on his scent. It meant that he could be one of those families that exclusively hunted dragons back when the magic ran wild over the land and humanity was just a thought in the minds of most magical creatures. It meant that particular family probably had more Dragon Stones, petrified remains of their children, in its grasp.

Following them and removing those vermin would be an act of war that would bring a united Fae nation against the dragon-kind, so for now he remembered the scent, the sight, and the magic of the one who had captured him. What most beings forgot was that through even eons, Dragons never forgot.

"Is it always so crowded?" Vulwin asked, pulling him from his musings. "I can scarcely move without bumping into someone."

"It's warm and not too humid for spring," Iffear explained. "There is no real horrible smell coming from the waters, there are several conventions running right now, and the children are still in school. Baltimore is waking up for the summer." He grinned at Vulwin. "And that means tourists, thieves, buskers, panhandlers, police chases, crime will rise, and the crazy people in this town will think it's just another day in Charm City."

"Charm City?" Vulwin looked around at the

architecture, a combination of gothic, Neo-classic, and modern with a raised eyebrow. "I guess you could call it that. How many gargoyles actually live in this town?" He noted a pair of abstract golden-tinted protectors guarding the front of a hotel and offered them a nod. Since their heads were unseeable, they wiggled their wings in his direction and the people passing by didn't even notice. "I guess you can call it charming."

"From a distance." Iffear laughed. "The locals call it Harm City and react accordingly. There is this awesome T-shirt I own with the words, 'Welcome to Baltimore… Now Duck, Motherfucker' printed across the front. It describes this city perfectly. Welcoming and dangerous. It is one of the reasons I love this town so much. Nothing really fazes these people."

"If all the human world was like this --"

"I'd murder them all," Iffear said with such certainty that Vulwin shot him a curious glance. "Really. It is fine in small doses, but such chaos needs to be contained. There is magic here that seems to draw its own back. They take a bit of themselves everywhere they go, which is why others from other lands give them distance until this land releases their hold on them. They should be fearful or angry coming from a place such as this, a place prone to violence and uproar, yet they are gleefully accepting. The magics of other places, other cities and lands barely affect them at all. They are chaos contained, and it needs to stay this way. If it spread out this human world would be in more danger of annihilation than it currently is."

"So… warrior magic?"

"So much blood has been spilled in this land -- human, Fae, Native to the land, foreign invaders… this land bleeds conflict, and that has affected its pull on its people. In small doses the people here are wonderful yet if their… magics, their essence, were to spread *en masse*, it would be too much chaos to contain."

"They are that connected to wild magic?" Vulwin asked. "Because what you are describing is what we call wild magic."

"Then yes, I am." Iffear tipped back his head and peered up at his mate. It was cute that Vulwin in either form was taller than him. It was adorable. He had rarely been the "little spoon," but his mate loved to wrap those long limbs of his around his body, as if he was touch starved and afraid that his comfort-dragon was going to disappear. Perhaps he wasn't used to comfort. It seemed that he and his father had a very odd relationship. It wasn't incestuous, but it seemed less than a paternal relationship among the Dhrow people should be.

"Then this appeals to you because Dragon-kind are closest to the wild magics of The Five."

"I would not disagree." Iffear reached up and tucked a strand of long silky hair behind his mate's tiny human ear, detangling it from his jewelry before he let his hand rest comfortably on his mate's neck.

Vulwin was bending over, bringing his full lips closer to his when instincts and maybe a tug from the land caught his attention.

He turned to the side in time to see a small wreck of a car speeding in their direction. They were on the sidewalk, a few feet away from their own car when he noticed the small hoopty was not slowing down and…

Instinct made him jerk them to the left. He cursed as they both fell, Iffear rolling so that his back ate up most of the impact of their fall. Ignoring the screams of the passersby and the growls of the gargoyles watching, Iffear wrapped most of his body around Vulwin and tucked them neatly against the base of the building. Clothing tore and the sharp smell of gasoline and engine exhaust filled his nostrils. The world spun for just a minute before there was an unholy crash, and the world seemed to suddenly speed up.

He could feel the heat around them, hear the shouts of those watching, feel his mate beneath him fall loose and limber in an attempt to connect to the land's magic and throw up some kind of barrier.

The sound of the crash filled the air for a moment, then silence filled the afternoon. A shrill scream drew his attention up, and Iffear opened eyes he had not remembered closing to see the cracked twisted metal of an engine block inches above their head.

"So, should your Welcome to Baltimore shirt also include tuck and roll?" his mate asked and Iffear resisted the urge to giggle like a child. "Because if this is the welcome I get to this city, I may want to rethink my living area."

Chapter Three

"Well," Vulwin said as they closed the door to his mate's home. "That was unique. A first for me, really... And now the reporters will swarm."

"But business will pick up," Mai pointed out, reaching down to stroke an agitated Chinsie. "And my photo broke on TMZ right before news of your accident, so double exposure."

Win wasn't lying. By the time they left the hospital after giving the police a report on the runaway car that somehow broke free from a tow truck and nearly mowed them over, the reporters were indeed swarming.

News of supermodel and celebrity spokesperson Win Arcarius' near-death experience after a designer photoshoot in Baltimore spread like wildfire and had reporters flocking to the small city on the Chesapeake Bay.

To get to their car, they'd had to run a gauntlet of reporters all thrusting mics in their faces and shouting questions. Words like "near-fatal" and "husband" made Vulwin want to laugh in their faces, but he preferred to keep his cool human facade in place. Near-fatal was laughable given their abilities, and the word "husband" was too weak a word to describe the ever-strengthening bond they had created.

They both sported bandages in obvious places; they had to pretend to be a little hurt from their brush with death. Vulwin decided to play it calm and unconcerned while Iffear took on the part of protective husband, guiding him through the reporters until Win stopped him to make a quick statement.

"Yes, I am married. It's legal in the United States but not everywhere in the world. Yes, this is my husband who saved my life and protected me from greater injury. No, I am not going to say more than that at this time. Thank you for your concern."

Then they hustled away to their waiting car that Mai had been all too happy to bring to Johns Hopkins Hospital, with an agitated Chinsie in the front seat.

As the doors opened, the sleek black cat leaped out to scramble up to Iffear's shoulders to sniff him over before turning her attention to Vulwin. The reporters there got lots of footage of the silky black kitty leaping into his arms and nuzzling at his chin. He cuddled her close as they made their way inside the car with Vulwin and Iffear riding in the back.

"What's the word?" Iffear had murmured to his cat as Mai skillfully weaved them in and out of traffic, eluding reporters and taking them home.

His familiar's soft voice filled both of their minds as she passed on the gathered intelligence. *"The word from the Gargoyles is that it was no accident. Fae magics were released and the car was guided in your direction."*

"Have I offended other Faes by moving into their territory without permission or a welcoming gift?" Win asked right off. He understood political maneuvering and wouldn't take it personally if he'd tripped up on protocol and was reminded to play nice.

"Not that I know of." Iffear wrinkled his cute little nose as he thought it over. "But I never had any issue moving in."

"You are a dragon, darling," Win pointed out, leaning over to kiss that cute little nose. "No one is going to fuck with you."

"I'll ask around." Chinsie seemed agitated. *"Someone must know if we stepped on any toes."*

"Wonderful," Win murmured, offering her his mental thanks. "Then we can fix the problem and move on. I've brought several good pieces of jewelry as trading gifts, as one never knows when one must make amends for a wrong."

"Sounds like that concept came from your father." Iffear kissed him back and gave him a smile.

"One of the only things that man has ever given me was the ability to follow the rules and know my place."

"Aren't you two cute, cooing at each other," Mai called from the front seat. "But keep your clothes on. This isn't a limo with a privacy screen, and unless I'm getting paid for it, I don't want to watch you two make out. At least without a camera I can set up to get some good shots."

"Mercenary little tramp, aren't you?" Vulwin laughingly called out to her.

"And that makes you like me more," she returned, chuckling.

And now they were all in Iffear's apartment, hoping to get a drink and calm down.

"What a beautiful introduction to your fair city," Win teased, and Iffear rolled his eyes as he made for the bedroom.

"I need a shower. I smell like busted old car and model."

"You like the smell of model!" Win called to his back. "And don't use up all the hot water. I smell like crotchety old tattoo artist."

Mai laughed at their antics before turning to face Win directly. "Really, are you okay?"

"I am fine," he assured her, pointing to the one bandage on his forehead. "A mere scrape."

"I tease a lot, but I care about the boss." She nibbled at her bottom lip for a moment before adding, "He means a lot to me. And by extension, you mean a lot to me. You make him... happy."

"He wasn't happy before?"

"He was more content," Mai decided. "He was content, but being content and being happy are two different things. He means a lot to me because he was willing to take a chance on me when I had almost nothing."

Win tilted his head to the side and got a good look, a really good look at Mai. She seemed sincere, her veneer of joking put aside as she spoke to him from the heart.

"I had no place to go and was really thinking about not so nice ways out. I had no family left, no real friends, no connections. I had a job that I loathed but couldn't leave and... life was shit, okay? Then I ran into this bald, musclebound, tatted guy who asked me if I wanted my ears pierced."

"Just like that?" Win questioned. He was learning more about the people in his mate's life, and he didn't want to forget a thing.

"No," she admitted, moving to one of the leather couches that dominated the blank wide space of the living room. "I saw some jewelry in his window. I was walking past after running some errand for my previous boss and... there were these earrings, just steel hoops with etchings, but I fell in love. I would pass this shop every day and stop and stare at them. It was embarrassing to be so drawn to something so insignificant, but something about them called to me. I stopped past every day that I could until one day they were just gone."

"Utterly frustrating," Win said in agreement with the expression on her face as he moved to sit beside her. Mai reached out and tugged at the torn T-shirt, frowning before pulling her attention back to his face.

"You have no idea. I think I wept a little. I was about to move on when the door opens, and this huge man held the door open for me. You better believe I walked right past him and back to my boss.

"This went on for about a month. I would walk past and peer into the window, hoping to see the earrings returned, but they never were. But the door would always open and I would always walk past. Finally, one day when the door opened, I asked why? Why was this man inviting me into his shop? It was obvious I didn't have money, and I know I looked a hot mess, but he just opened the door. I told him if he was going to rape and kill me, he was going about it the wrong way because no career criminal would invite a knowing victim into their murder chamber. That was the first time I heard Iffear laugh."

Mai grinned at the recollection. "He told me if he wanted to rape and kill me, all's he had to do was pluck my short ass off the street. Instead he wanted to know if I wanted my ears pierced. I asked him why, and he said a tattoo shop was much cleaner than a novelty shop or a franchise store. I told him I didn't have any money and he told me he didn't ask about that. He wanted to know if I wanted my ears pierced. I was going to walk away, but Chinsie came out and was winding between his legs. She jumped up on his shoulder and nuzzled him, and then I knew he was safe. Animals... People don't pay enough attention to animals. She was telling me it was okay to trust him a little. I went in and he pierced my ears with those same earrings I was going crazy over."

Mai pulled her 'fro up to expose the tips of her ears and there, set in pure silver, were hoops etched in ancient protection runes. She fluffed her hair back in place and turned to grin at him.

"It was so easy, and it made me feel... safe, I guess. And then I realized that I wanted to make others feel the same way. I realized I had self-worth and that I didn't need to be stuck where I was, living for scraps of kindness only to get more abuse than acceptance. I went home, told my boss off, and came right back here. Iffear offered to teach me how to pierce and offered me a place to stay on the second floor of this building. I took a chance and I learned. And now the second floor is mine." She giggled. "I live there paying rent with three of the seven tattoo artists who live here. The top two floors belong to the boss and though we visit sometimes, he keeps mainly to himself. He was lonely. We could tell. And now he's not so lonely. He went on vacation and came back with a husband, and I've never seen him happier."

"That is a lot," Win began, smiling at the many acts of kindness perpetuated by his mate. The earrings, the protective charms placed on them that would embolden the wearer to speak up for themselves and dispel any negative energy about them... Offering her and the unspoken others who he probably helped in some way, who now worked for him and lived in his human den... Iffear was amazing.

"I don't know why I told you all that," Mai continued. "Unless it was to let you know that Iffear Draconis is really loved here. We want the best for him and from the way he looks at you, it appears you are the best."

"Well, I hope to be." Vulwin gave her honesty in return, fair trade. "What is happening between us... it happened so fast, but it feels so good and so right."

Win thought about that for a moment and realized each word spoken was the fullest truth he had ever spoken.

"It feels right to both of us. Iffear feels like home. I don't think I ever want to leave his side. I want to make him happy. I want to lavish the things he loves on him, even if I don't quite understand all what that is. I want to see him smile, hear him laugh... I want to make him proud every time I step out of our house. I want him to never regret taking a chance with me."

Almost as if popping out of a spell, he blinked away his romantic thoughts and offered Mai a wry grin. "I just want him happy." That kind of honesty took a lot out of a being, he decided as he slumped a bit on the couch.

"Good," Mai chirped happily. "That means I don't have to cut ya!"

Mai and Vulwin were still laughing when Iffear returned from his shower. Threats of violence and politics, those were things that Vulwin knew and appreciated. It made him accept Mai as one of his, and those who belonged to him, like Chinsie, like Iffear -- they always deserved his most honest best.

Besides, the little bloodthirsty human was fun.

Iffear stared at them as they rolled around on the couch like children, before he shook his head in dismay. "What have I gotten myself into?"

His muttered words made them laugh all the harder.

* * *

It woke him up in the middle of the night... the calling.

Iffear's eyes snapped open as he slowly unwound himself from his mate. Vulwin was back in his Dhrow form, all long, dark, speckled skin and huge eyes, wasted from the sex they'd just had.

Vulwin was a masterful lover and claimed that all his experience came from being on the bottom for most of his sexual life. Iffear ran his gaze over Win's warm naked body, noting the cock ring that still encircled the base of his dick. It was a beautiful filigree and enhanced the looks of his already pretty cock. Vulwin as a lover was perfectly expressive, and had no qualms about asking for what he wanted or telling Iffear what he wanted to do to him. Iffear, being quite a bit older than his lover, was content to let him explore and experience a different side of lovemaking. Just that night, they'd traded off being on the bottom until sheer exhaustion drove them to damn near pass out in the sheets. But it wasn't soreness that brought Iffear to sudden awareness.

There was a feeling, a tug that he had only felt once before. It wasn't as strong, but yes, there was that feeling again. Someone was trying to lure… him?

"What the fuck?" His hissed words jolted Vulwin from his deep sleep, and huge black-and-silver eyes stared at him in question.

"Magic," Vulwin spoke softly. "Someone is working something… arcane…"

Vulwin sat up, the loose braid he kept his hair in for sleeping settled down around his chest as he yawned, wiping at his eyes.

If the matter of magic wasn't so urgent Iffear would have pulled him back into the bed and kissed the adorableness right off of his face.

"Arcane?" he asked, tossing the sheets aside and rising to his feet.

The half-moon cast bright bars of light across their bed. Looking up through the massive skylight on their ceiling, Iffear saw thousands of stars twinkling against the purple black velvet of the night sky, gleaming like the marks that peppered his mate's skin. He felt more than heard Vulwin rise to stand next to him before he wrapped those long, soft-skinned arms around him. For a moment he felt he'd pulled some of the majesty of the beautiful night sky from the heavens and bundled it around himself in perfect form to make him feel safe. Because the lure got stronger, and the emotions running through him were terrifying.

"It's a dragon-stone," he murmured, and Vulwin nodded his head in agreement, pressing a kiss to the back of his neck as he lowered his head. "I can feel it. I can feel its draw."

"Has such a thing happened before?" Vulwin's deep voice was soft, offering a measure of comfort as shudders began to rack his body.

"Not here, never here. I would have felt it and dealt with it before now. Maybe this is what has the wild magics stirred up," Iffear mused. "Someone is playing with death magic; someone has a dragon soul... a murdered baby, in their grasp. I can feel it screaming in agony, Vulwin. It is begging for help. It is begging for true death."

Iffear sniffed, fighting back tears as he pictured the small seed of life, pictured the tiny slip of promise of life fighting in its amber prison. Not understanding anything but the pain it was in, since something yanked it from the comfortable and safe womb of its egg. He could feel its fear, its confusion, its clear lack of understanding as to what was going on. It was in agony, and its pain called to him.

"It is suffering," Iffear whispered and felt his mate's arms tighten around him. "It's so lost and afraid --"

"Then we shall go and free it." The words spoken were all-powerful, as if Vulwin had spoken it into being the truth. They were princely in their form and defiance of fate; they were spoken as if it had already been done, that him mentioning it was just being polite for politeness' sake.

Iffear stepped back and turned to look at his mate and through his anguish, a smile broke free. He was looking at the battle strategist and warrior Vulwin had proven himself to be centuries ago. The look of sheer determination on his face said that he would have his way, that his will would not be denied.

Vulwin tepped away, snapped his fingers, and almost instantly a trunk appeared out of thin air beside him. "Those who practice such abominations have no right to take one iota of life this world has to offer. Those who practice such things should be snuffed out, hidden from the light, and made to repent before they cease to be. I will ensure that this is thus, my mate. On this, you have my word."

As he spoke, Vulwin dressed himself in tight black pants and an equally form-fitting black tunic. Over that went a sleeveless ebony gambeson, the dark black leather layered with silk and animal skins melded to the shape of his body, providing protection and freedom of movement. The rich expensive leather armor fell to the top of his thighs, held in place with a wide black belt that held a sheathed dagger on the right side and an elegant war blade of Dhrovish design on the left. Just behind the sword rested a quiver that seemed to pulse with magic. Iffear stared at it and swore he could only see thirty or so arrows resting there in clusters of twelve, but he gave it a second look and the number of fletched arrows seemed to triple. Magic space, he decided as Vulwin waved his hands again and thigh-high leather boots appeared around his legs. The soft, supple leather encased his legs beautifully, providing protection and freedom of movement that he would need as an archer. Another wave of magic conjured beautiful embroidered shin guards. They were buckled tight around his calves, and the protection runes etched into them flashed silver for a moment before it faded to a deep black.

Iffear was content to watch as his mate dressed himself for war, slinging an embroidered leather wrist guard onto his right arm, then a set of finger tabs onto his left hand, the leather gloves covering his three middle fingers while leaving his pinky and thumb bare, so he could easily grip and carry things. A dark, knee-length hooded cloak went over all that, and then he pulled from the trunk one of the deadliest looking recursive bows Iffear had ever seen.

The upper and lower limbs were made from delicately curved blackwood, while the nocks, the arched tips that held the boosting in place, were made of a dark ebony material that seems to absorb the light. The grip and arrow rest were made from the same material as the nocks, designed to fit Vulwin's left hand perfectly. There was no visible string, but when Win's right hand plucked at the space where a string would be, a fine black line shimmered into existence.

"The string is magic?" Iffear asked, taking in the whole of his mate. The warrior looked like a dark shadow, most of his body hidden in black cloth and leather. He could easily see the Dhrow slipping in and out of dark places, undetected, to wreak vengeance and death upon all he deemed unworthy.

"My life-force." Vulwin grinned, his sharp teeth gleaming whitely in the dimness of his room. He looked like a dark wraith. "Aren't you going to get ready?"

Iffear rolled his eyes. "Pompous Dhrows," he sniffed, then walked over to his chest of drawers and pulled out leather pants and a tight T-shirt.

Vulwin stared at him in confusion as he donned his chosen attire and sat on the bed to pull on the boots his lover had gifted him with before they left for human territory.

"Is that all you are wearing?" In comparison to what his mate was wearing, Iffear appeared woefully underdressed.

"Dragon," Iffear reminded him, rising to his feet. He lifted both hands before him, and with a pull of his innate magic, both hands were engulfed black flame. "Odd." He carefully examined the flames in one hand, bringing them up to the level of his eyes. "My flames used to be green." If he looked carefully enough... yes, there was a slice of green, but it was quickly swallowed up by the black. No, not swallowed up, encased.

"My bad," Vulwin admitted, tossing his bow onto the bed before walking closer and carefully caging Iffear's hand between his own. "Dhrovish protective magic. All that I am and what I will ever become is extended to my mate. Which means my invulnerability, at the moment, is extended to you."

"You made me invulnerable?"

"To most things, but that's just a layer of magic covering your own. Your own magic is still there. It's just now being carefully guarded, and I carefully guard everything that is mine."

"So, I am yours?" Iffear asked, arching one eyebrow as he extinguished his fames.

Immediately Vulwin gripped his hand and pulled it to his face, nuzzling into the palm before he placed a gentle kiss there. "And I belong to you," his mate intoned seriously. "All your problems are now my problems. All your joys are now my joys. All your pain is my anguish and all that delights you brightens my heart."

Each word was true. Iffear could feel it in his soul. Each word that his mate spoke was true and he believed.

"Now come. Let me ease your heart, my Dragon," his Dhrow purred. "Let us lay your kin to rest."

Chapter Four

It took mere moments for them to exit the brownstone on Water Street and follow the path of distressed magic to the Pagoda at Patterson Park.

The night was unusually quiet for the busy city. There were still the usual assorted club goers and those who inhabited the after-hour spots that dotted the city, but for the most part, it was unnaturally quiet.

They made their way swiftly down Baltimore Street, invisible to most whom they passed, pausing to nod at the gargoyles that dotted the city as they rapidly flew toward the waiting power until they reached the park.

Other than a few people obviously up to no good hiding in the shadows, the park was clear of human life.

"This is the place?" Vulwin asked. He had been diligently following his mate through the city and its strange people and shops. The night air was a bit humid, but that was accepted as the city was situated at the mouth of a bay.

"It is." Iffear was not winded at all, and in fact moved through the people so swiftly on wings of magic that at times he was a blur even to Vulwin's magical eyes.

"It's beautiful." Vulwin nodded, squatting down and touching the soft green grass under a tree, mere feet away from the towering gold-and-brown pagoda situated in the center of the park. "In the middle of all this glass and concrete and metal, there is a place where nature prevails."

"There are several parks," Iffear said absently as he looked around the area. "I'll show them to you sometime."

Vulwin rose to his feet, following his mate, who now looked as if he were in a daze. "Iffear?"

"So much pain," he whispered, turning to follow a path that led to a wooden walkway nearly hidden in tall decorative reeds. "Can't you feel it?"

Vulwin closed his eyes and tried to concentrate on the link he shared with his dragon. In his mind's eye, their bond was a heavy golden thread that connected the two of them. He could see his dark earth magic coating the bond with its protection and Iffear's green... life energy? He didn't know. He would have to ask about the element that Iffear's magic centered on, but it was a pulsing, living thing that seemed to throb with life and vitality. He could follow those green threads back to himself where they comfortably entwined with his earth magic. It was these green threads that he concentrated on.

There was happiness, he was proud to see. And confusion. That was to be expected. There was a new bond under unusual circumstances, after all. There was a lust for life and curiosity about what seemed to be everything, and intelligence that Iffear didn't see the need to brag about... and there... There was a pulse of sickly yellow tugging at the green threads.

He reached out to touch and hissed as he drew back. There was such anguish and agony... How could any being do this to another and still stay sane? How was it that Iffear wasn't burning everything in this park to ash?

"Because it would destroy innocence."

Vulwin opened his eyes to see his mate standing before him, his red eyes blazing as he stared intently into his own.

"I could never be responsible for taking away innocent life, Vulwin. Going on a rampage would only destroy the trees and grass here, which would harm the birds and small mammals that make the park home. Left unchecked, my flame would travel to the homes that border this park on the eastern side, contaminate the small creeks that run here, and snuff out any creature who happened to witness my rage. I could not live with that on my conscience."

Vulwin nodded in understanding. He was a creature of death. Death he understood and held no fear of. You killed things and they returned to the earth from whence they came. Death was a familiar and close friend. Yet from Iffear's point of view, life was just as much of an ally as death. Where Vulwin was trained in taking life, Iffear seemed to be more concerned with nurturing and protecting it.

"That's why dragons make such perfect parents and protectors." Vulwin leaned down and pressed a kiss to his mate's lips. "And that is why this must be killing you inside."

"You recognize the magic?" Iffear asked, curiosity on his face even as he winced and pulled back from Vulwin. "You can feel it?" He looked around the park, his gaze going deeper along the bordered wooden path.

"Yes." Win turned to follow the where his mate's eyes were following. "It is a corrupt, nasty thing, and I can feel the pain of the trapped being."

"You know what dragon-stones are." Iffear began to move down that path. "And now you know why they are used to lure us."

"To right the wrong, to free the life trapped within."

"To ease the suffering of the unborn and deliver it peace."

Quietly, Vulwin moved beside his mate, letting

him take the lead and follow the corrupted magic to the source.

It didn't take them long at all. In fact, it was stupidly easy to find the trio of short men who leaned against a picnic table at the end of the path where it emptied into a small, hilly field.

All three were dressed in black and green, wearing hoodies and baseball caps as they paid almost no attention to what was going on around them.

As Vulwin and Iffear watched from the shadows of a large tree, a human rode a bike up to the three, and after a muted conversation and a few furtive looks around them, the human handed over some cash and the pixies handed over a small bag of white powder.

The human disappeared just as rapidly, and the trio, almost as one, turned to face them.

"We know... you... there," the tallest of the three commented. "Can feel... magic."

Motioning for Vulwin to stay back, Iffear moved slowly forward until he stood before the three.

Softly hissing his displeasure, Vulwin pulled a cluster of arrows from his quiver, stabbing them into the ground before him as he pulled his bow from his shoulder. These particular arrows were made of yew, the heads made of silver dipped in the juice of rowan berries. They would be painful if not deadly to most Fae who played in the human realm. If one of them made a wrong move...

"Why do you lure me?" Iffear demanded, his eyes glowing red. The pale light of the half-moon lightened the area to a dim dark purple and lengthened the shadows of the trees that surrounded them. It was a perfect night for an archer to pick off targets.

"Lure? We three? Would do that?" they hissed in

unison, their screeching voices carrying over to Win in the stillness of the night.

"You know what you do, what you have?"

"Trinket?" The tallest giggled. "The trinket. You want. How much you pay?"

"Pay?" Iffear hissed.

"Money we need," they chorused together, concentrating solely on Iffear. Maybe their combined magics blocked his presence from their sight. Maybe they appeared as one? Vulwin didn't know, but he blessed whatever fates decided to keep their attention solely on his mate. It left him free to attack. He placed an arrow on the arrow rest and drew back his bow.

"Human money?" Iffear sniffed. "Don't make me laugh. You don't need human money. Besides, you are selling them drugs."

"Drugs?" the chided. "No. We sell… happiness."

"In powder form." The tallest and their apparent leader giggled.

"Pixie dust will rot a human's brain," Iffear growled. "It leaves them pixilated and unable to see what their life's path should be."

"Not unable," the leader argued as the other two grumbled. "Detoured."

All three cackled and Iffear took an angry step forward.

"No. Dragon, are you?" The tallest stepped back, the other two following as he pulled a chain from around his neck. "They said would bring dragon, yes?"

At the end of the metal chain hung an amber-colored jeweled, the size of the palm of Vulwin's hand. It was a dragon-stone, this one larger than the one he'd sung to rest at his home.

Immediately Iffear's eyes were drawn to it, almost as if his consciousness was trapped by the glittering orb.

"Need human money. Like human things," the three sang out, the sound of their voices growing sharp enough to send shivers down Vulwin's spine.

"Was said this would lure," the tallest purred. "Was said dragon have human money." Then his voice turned so shrill it felt as if blades were jabbing into Vulwin's ears. "Maybe... we like Dragon hide more... dragon eyes... dragon skin..."

Iffear was trapped, unmoving, his eyes glued to the swinging pendant that glittered almost menacingly in the light of the moon as the pixie reached out toward him. Vulwin could feel a sudden distress in their bond before he let the first arrow fly.

The tallest pixie squealed, gripping his hand as the arrow embedded itself through his palm. The second shot severed the chain and had the amulet dropping to the ground as all three turned to search the shadows for him, the tallest still screaming in distress.

The hypnotic hold broken, Iffear threw back his head and roared as he raced forward. Vulwin let loose another arrow, this one striking the pixie to the left in center mass before he reached for another arrow.

Iffear thrust one arm out, throwing out a small, controlled ball of fire as the pixies separated, dropping their product, each flying off in a different direction, shaking off the forms they chose and shrinking down until they were the size of large rats. Yes, they *were* rats, vermin who preyed on those less fortunate than themselves. They were rats that needed to be exterminated.

The wind began to whip the trees into a frenzy as Vulwin grabbed up his arrows and charged toward his mate and those who would do him harm. Holding three arrows in one hand, he lined up and fired at one fleeing Fae as Iffear threw flames at the other two. He heard a squeal and knew that at least one of his arrows flew true.

In their real form, pixies were like miniature Elvhen folk, delicate-looking and slim, with pointed ears and huge, tilted eyes. But they came in the bright colors of the flora usually found on earth, bright green and happy yellows. The one he'd struck mid- air was bloodred and hissing as he reached its side and stared down at the malicious thing.

A flinch from its impaled body sent the grass bursting into growth, turning into tendrils and wrapping around Vulwin's legs. Vulwin didn't panic. He even glared at the sprite as he waved his hand, and the earth sucked the grass back down to its natural length, pulling the pixie magic out of the soil.

A gust of wind blew the hood of his cloak back from his face and exposed him to the now gasping sprite. "Dhrow!" it hissed before Vulwin stabbed an arrow through its heart.

"You attacked my mate!" was the last thing the pixie heard before life fled its body and its physical form exploded into ash.

"Return to the earth," Vulwin murmured, offering a small prayer before turning to see what was happening to his mate.

Iffear had the other two pixies trapped in a black ring of fire. The larger one with the injured hand was the color of moss while the second frantically fluttering pixie was bright fuchsia, the color of the sky at sunset. He walked closer, bow and arrow in hand, listening to the hissed conversation.

"You go!" the injured green pixie was hissing. "You attack! We defend!"

"You lured me from my home to what? Harvest dragon parts?" Iffear chided. "Stupid, stupid pixies. Who told you it would be that easy?"

The two miniature Fae stared at each other for a moment before they began to hiss and curse. "You have no right!"

"Your compatriot is dead." Vulwin's sudden appearance seemed to shock the two into silence. "He died proclaiming what I am. Do you know what I am?"

"Dhrow," the injured one hissed. "Walking death. Tyrant! Saboteur!"

"Archer," Vulwin added, drawing back on his magical string after setting an arrow in its rest. "One who can take his time shooting off parts of you until you are nothing more than a miserable babbling ball of flesh on the ground."

Silence fell and Iffear tightened the ring of fire, making the circle of space they inhabited smaller.

"Give it to me," his mate growled.

"Dragon... cherish life!" the injured pixie called out.

"Dhrow cherishes dragons," Vulwin shot back in their own cadence. "And this particular Dhrow is not at all pleased that you had plans to butcher my mate!"

"Take!" the Pixy squealed after hearing that. "Take! Take! Take!"

"Not playing that game," Iffear snarled. "I've been around your kind long enough to know that when you go bad you excel at playing word games that hurt or carry curses. Make your words clear."

"They say dragons no understand," the pink one hissed, his eyes still on Vulwin who cheerfully added another arrow to the rest and nodded to Iffear.

"I bet you, my dragon, that I can remove both feet with the same shot."

"Word it clearly," Iffear demanded, eyes on the moss green pixie.

"They say dragon stupid…" he muttered again.

"Who?" Vulwin wanted to know.

"Elvhen," they spat together and Vulwin rolled his eyes.

"You believe that shit from the early dragon wars?" He laughed. "Don't you know that the Elvhen almost got their asses burned out of existence for that crap? And you were going to do what? Lure him here for dragon parts?"

"Black market," the pink one hissed, and Iffear tightened the ring again, making it so small that the two pixies were pressing close to each other to prevent being scorched by Dragon Fire.

"I bet you're worth more in parts than whole," Vulwin teased his mate. "At least you are a lot less dangerous that way."

But Iffear was not in a joking mood. "You know what I want. Name it. Give it to me clearly."

"The stone," the green one squealed. "Untethered, it belongs to you!"

"Thank you." Iffear offered them a smile before snapping the ring closed and popping off both of their obnoxious heads. Another small ball of fire incinerated the small packages the pixies had been peddling to the humans.

Shrugging at his mate's actions, Vulwin returned his arrows to their quiver and moved to embrace his mate. For a moment, Iffear stood stiffly in his arms, then he relaxed by degrees. Vulwin could still feel the lure pulling at him with their bond, but the unnatural pull was lessened now that the pixie magic was dissipating.

"Are you okay?" he finally asked as the moon's

light began to wane. Dawn was fast approaching, and they still had unfinished business.

"No," Iffear finally spoke, his voice nearly incomprehensible with anguish. "I can still hear the screams of that unborn soul. It needs to be put to rest."

Vulwin pulled away from Iffear and plodded back to where the chain with the dragon-stone lay glistening in the grass. He picked it up, cupping it carefully in his hand, before bringing it up to his heart.

"I -- we can sing it to rest," Vulwin offered, feeling his own heart burn in sorrow as he felt the screams and fear of the unhatched soul. "I -- I --"

"It can't be done now, I know." Iffear turned to lean against his mate. "In the Gray Gulf where we are constantly surrounded by magic, it would be possible. But here in the human realm, we must wait until the convergence of day and night, of life and death to see this soul passed safely unto the next realm."

"Sunset," Vulwin agreed. "We can do it at sunset. Do you have a place in mind?"

"I have a rooftop garden." Iffear pulled back from his mate. "We can do it there. Until then, I will offer this lost one what comfort I can."

Vulwin held up the broken chain and with a wave of magic, Iffear repaired the pewter links so that Iffear could loop the amulet around his neck, resting the jewel comfortably against his heart.

"Let's go home, my dragon," Vulwin urged, running his hands up and down his mate's arms. "Let me take you home."

* * *

Back at home, Iffear couldn't wait to strip out of his clothes and toss them in a corner and just shower.

He turned the water as hot as it could go and just stood under the showerhead, letting streams of scalding water flow over his body.

His heat had long passed and his bond with his Dhrow was settling nicely, yet his heart burned. It was true that the water made him yearn for an egg to hatch, for a youngling created from him and his powerful mate, but that was not what this pain was about.

His mind and his heart ached at the useless slaughter of innocence. What kind of being did one have to be to crack open a stolen egg and rip from it a soul yet not ready to be fully formed in the visage of its creators? What kind of disrespect for life must one have to steal it away before it actually came to be?

He tried to comfort the trapped soul as best he could, but it was too immature, its brain not yet fully developed. All it knew was pain and agony, and nothing would fix that until they were able to sing it back into the earth and set the trapped soul free.

If he were a different person, he would have long since gone rogue and murdered all the Elvhen race. Suddenly he understood the insanity and the anger of his past ancestors when they instigated the Dragon Wars. Suddenly he understood the desire to unmake all that went into creating such a foul species.

In his head he knew that not all the Fae-folk were the same, but his heart screamed out for vengeance for those who needlessly tortured and corrupted. How many more dragon-stones were out there? How many of his kind were trapped in anguish, fear, and pain? How many more would be used to lure his kind into their own demise?

"Dragon parts," he muttered. To some, that was all he was worth. A collection of body parts and magic that could be used to wreak havoc and destruction when ill magic was applied.

The steam turned the air white and cloudy, and

he inhaled deeply, hoping it would somehow cleanse his soul of the vicious thoughts that were circulating. How he would love to find them, devour them, burn them into ash! How he would love to destroy them, their land, their allies, and anyone who had ever done anything for them until the very word "Elvhen" would send listeners scurrying into the shadows, afraid of what would befall them for uttering that forbidden, awful name.

"My dragon."

Iffear jerked as long arms wrapped around his body, pulling him back into a taller muscular frame. Almost as if conjured out of the misty air, his mate was there, wrapping him in safety and comfort.

"What distresses you so?" Vulwin asked as his hands ran over Iffear's arms before they pulled him tighter to the Dhrow's solid chest. "This?"

His fingers made their way up to cup the hand Iffear had fisted about the stone.

"This, we can set right," Vulwin whispered into his ear, his shower-wet hair falling around them. "This we can fix. We can ease this wee one into the next dimension with all the grace and respect it deserves. What we can't do is stop the magic that created this. There are only a few who know what a dragon-stone is, let alone how to create one, and most of them have passed far beyond our reach."

"It's an un-death," Iffear gasped, tears filling his eyes. The screams of the trapped soul eased as his mate offered him compassion and safety. The feel of it must be getting through to the trapped soul.

"Now death I understand, my dragon. Half death, full death, near death... There is only one way to combat death. That is with understanding, acceptance, and with life."

"Life stops death?" Iffear tilted his head up and to the side to peer at the large, bi-colored eyes glinting down at him.

"Not just life," his mate explained in his Dhrovish way. "Celebrating life. Celebrating all that it is and what it means to be alive."

"Eat, drink, and be merry?"

"Eat, drink, fuck, laugh, love, cry, rant, rage… all these things make up life. Humans have named emotions as negative and positive. How stupid is that? How can you not know what happiness is unless you have sadness to compare it to? How can you understand death without first living life? Emotions are just… emotions. There is no good or bad without them. They are just there. There is no good or bad in feeling the way you do now, my dragon. You feel. And that is more than enough to counter the corruption that seeks to enter your soul."

"This is the corruption." Iffear narrowed his eyes at his mate as he hefted the stone. "This abomination --"

"Can be fixed, can be healed. A life was lost and it can never be replaced, but we can balance out its loss by taking on the burden of living the life it should have had for it. We live for it, my mate. We fight, and we laugh, and we love, and we cry for it."

"And that would ease the corruption in my soul?" he asked, curious about what his lover would say.

"There is no corruption in your soul. It seeks to enter your soul and you are too strong to give it leave, my dragon, but you are grieving."

"Grieving, huh?" Iffear released the necklace and slowly turned in his mate's arms, ignoring the pain as the necklace settled against his wet chest.

"You grieve." Callused hands ran over his face swiping water away, hands that had just destroyed life with no regret for his cause. Those very same hands that could and would kill to defend now gently cupped his face as the black-and-silver eyes that he had come to cherish peered at him through the steam. "You didn't have time to grieve for one of your line, and now there is another small soul crying out for freedom. You are grieving what they could have been, my dragon. You are grieving their lack of existence, grieving the fact that there is nothing you can do to correct this issue and restore their lives to what they could have been. You grieve because you are a wonderful, beautiful, compassionate being who treats life with the respect it deserves. You are amazing, my love, and it is so amazing to someone like me who respects death more than life most days."

"Liar," Iffear hissed as the heat from his mate's body seemed to surround him. "You value life, my stubborn Dhrow. You value life as much as I. Otherwise, I would not be mated to you. If you had not accepted me, claimed me, taken me as your mate, I am quite sure I would have ended up as a pile of dragon parts in some Elvhen lab."

"Never." Vulwin rested his head against Iffear's as he pressed his body solidly against his dragon. "Chinsie would have murdered them all, and you would have simply walked away, stone in hand."

"As if I am that powerful --"

"You are mysterious magic, my mate." Vulwin's hand slid down to cup his ass, pulling him tightly against the bulge of his hardening cock. "You have the power to bring this Dhrovish prince to his knees."

Iffear groaned as he felt weakness swamp his body. His mate felt so damn good. He ran his hands up

Vulwin's body to cup his face, urging Win lower as he went up on his toes to press his lips gently against Win's. Win swallowed Iffear's moan and slid his tongue between Iffear's lips.

The taste of his mate nearly drove Iffear insane. Win tasted of spice and earth, and eager life. Iffear closed his eyes and lost himself in his mate's arms as Vulwin's fingers danced over his back, sliding down to cup his ass and slide over the hidden opening in the cleft of his ass.

Iffear moaned and pressed back against that teasing finger…

"Iffear?" Vulwin's voice was raised in fear and the sound of it showed and echoed around Iffear's head. God, he was so blissed out, gone on his mate, and the world was spinning and whirring and…

He never realized when his tentative hold on his consciousness disappeared or when he collapsed into a boneless heap in his mate's arms. All he could ever recall was struggling to breathe in the steamy room and the beautiful sound of his lover calling his name.

Chapter Five

"Iffear!" Vulwin knew his voice was filled with pain and anguish, but he couldn't really give a shit. Something was wrong with his mate.

One moment he was arching against him mewling so sweetly, calling out to him, and in the next... Thank the Five for his warrior reflexes, because his mate could have cracked his skull open on the stone floor of his shower as he fell.

And now, despite the heat in the steamy room, his dragon was shuddering as if he were encased in ice. Through the steam Vulwin could see Iffear's muscles seizing and trying to spasm off of his bones.

He had never seen Iffear in his dragon form, but the way his body was flexing, it was clear that he wasn't fully human. There were now bulges where there should be none and the feel of all that shifting beneath his skin...

"Fuck, Iffear!" he called again, giving him little shake and watched with fear crawling up his throat as his dragon's head listed weakly to the side.

He panicked. He could admit it. For a moment he panicked. He wanted to shake his lover, to force him to wake up, to open those beautiful red eyes and glare at him for his stupidity... but none of that was happening, and Iffear was growing colder in his arms.

The sudden drop in the dragon's body temperature pulled him out of his shock and forced him to act.

Vulwin hefted his mate in his arms and kicked through the glass shower door. He ignored the pinging of the glass breaking and the pain in his slashed feet as he strode through the glass and to the bedroom.

He placed Iffear onto the bed, and a wave of his

hand had warm air surrounding them both, drying away the water in an attempt to remove anything that would steal more of his precious body heat.

That done, he swaddled his dragon in as many blankets as he could conjure or find. If the heat was leaving the body, he needed to replace it and try to maintain it.

Vulwin was no healer, but he was going to use what he knew to do something. He could not let his mate falter like this. What the hell was this? How could he fix this? This wasn't right.

Naked and damp, he crouched over the cocoon he had made of Iffear, running his hands over his lover's face, trying to determine what was wrong.

This could not be happening, should not be happening. Iffear was his true mate, bounded and sealed by the Five Fates. The protection afforded to him should apply to his mate. His mate was not human, female, or pregnant. Nothing should be able to harm him. Hell, he hadn't even reached his Dhroven maturity, so anything short of a willingly accepted curse wouldn't even put a dent in those protections.

What had those damn pixies done? It had to be something they did as they died... maybe a death curse... No, that would not pierce his protections. Even if the spiteful pixies had tried to use their death as energy to power a curse, it would not have taken because they were in the wrong. They'd broken the faith by attacking...

None of this made any damn sense!

"Fuck!" he shouted, running his hands through this hair, jerking at its loose white strands. He was a fucking warrior. What the hell did he know about healing?

"Think, fool," he hissed at himself, squeezing his

eyes shut and knocking both fists into his forehead as his lover convulsed beneath him.

Before the pixies, their bond read clear and true… powerful… and… his head jerked up and he cursed softly at his own stupidity. "Read the fucking bond, you twat!"

Closing his eyes, he concentrated on that thread of magic that connected the two of them, pulled in on the essence of the bond… and jerked back, falling off the bed and onto the floor, trying his best not to retch all over the white carpet.

Pain. Overwhelming pain filled him as nausea and stole his breath. His whole body convulsed once before he managed to gain control of himself. There was a sickly yellow wrongness there, someone perverting their bond, trying its best to eat away at the green of his dragon's life energy. The black of his protections seemed to have faded to a gray and was growing weaker by the second.

Vulwin pulled the image of the bond once again to his mind's forefront. Now braced and having something to fight settled him. He was a warrior. Fighting was one thing he understood almost as much as he understood death. The sickly yellow… curse… had to have come from somewhere and that meant that he could track it.

Curling up on his side, he concentrated his rage on that yellow blob, that hungry thing that was consuming magic like a leech. It was crawling up the threads of their bond from Iffear's link, but how?

Sucking in a deep breath he plunged himself into the core of that yellow and found himself unable to prevent himself from spewing out his supper. It was malignant, insidious, and nasty, this curse. It was drawing power from Iffear's life, which made it incredibly strong, and it was eating rapidly away at the protections his mate's very nature afforded their bond, siphoning them off. He gagged again, but managed to take control of himself enough to follow the trail of destruction this curse wrought.

Painfully, one inch at a time, he divided the threads of their bond, pushing aside his own silvery black magic and the tugging at the weakening green of his mate's. He pushed aside several threads that he had not taken the time to recognize, the pink of empathy, the gold of intelligence, the light blue of growing love, and the blue of… love?

Everything around him stilled and it was like the magical plane was holding its breath as Vulwin plucked at the thickening blue thread. It was beautiful, sparkling in its truth. It was thin but growing thicker ever second he beheld its majesty. There was love, true love, staring him in the face and it… it gave him pause. It made him think.

He was… in love. It wasn't lust or curiosity or desire; this was the true-blue thing. He was holding love in his metaphysical hands. Almost lovingly he traced its roots, following the thread back to its origins, and yes… it was not one sided. The blue thread started in the heart of his own magic where it was thick and proud… and his mate's, it reached from the very core of him, growing and bubbling, flowing to meet in the middle where they eagerly merged, blending together, creating a solid pillar of strength that even the sickly yellow could not touch.

He loved his dragon, his mate, his Iffear… and it looked as if that love was returned in full measure. His mate loved him. He was beautiful and thoughtful, and oh so wise, and giving and accepting, and protective, and Iffear loved him. Him. The lost child that no one really gave a damn about beyond the position he was born into and his ability to snuff the life that fought to maintain its existence. The unwanted prince, the spy in human guise, the one they respected out of fear... was finally loved.

"Iffear," he moaned, clinging to that thread, watching as it grew thicker in his hands even as his love's life force was waning.

No. He would not let that happen. He would not let the one good thing to happen in his hellishly long life slip away through his fingers. No. He would save his love, save his dragon. And those who tried to harm him had better recognize that they just made an enemy that nothing in their power could ever hope to match or dominate.

He caressed that blue thread once more before releasing it and diving directly into the tangled yellow that was sapping his lover's life. Ruthlessly, he began to snatch at it, tearing it away from what was good and pure. He hacked at it, jerked it, strangled it until he could find a clear path back to where it originated from.

The closer he got to the heart of it, the more he began to hear... screams. Yes, there was screaming and crying, there was pain and anguish and he was getting two... emotions? One was trapped, screaming for release from the pain, the other was... hungry. He delved deeper and realized that the pain felt familiar... It was the pain emanating from the unborn soul trapped in the dragon-stone. That was expected, what they could fix, but the other...

He pulled back as realization slammed into him. The dragon-stone. It had been gifted freely without artifice. It had been accepted willingly and the burden laid next to his dragon's heart. It fit. It was the only thing that could eat away at his protections, a poison willingly accepted.

He jerked back to reality to see Chinsie sitting on the lump of Iffear, chirping and crooning softly to him while a hand stroked the hair back from his face. He looked up and saw that Mai was there, her brown eyes glittering black as she washed away the vomit from around his mouth and pulled a blanket tighter over him.

"Mai --" he croaked, confused and shocked at the same time. He wasn't in human guise and she wasn't reacting in any strange way. She didn't even look human, with those huge, tilted eyes and her skin that was slowly darkening until it was nearly as dark as his own. "Brownie," he gasped, and she offered him a smile filled with some of the sharpest, most dangerous teeth he had ever seen -- and he'd fought orcs and trolls.

"That I am." She snapped her fingers, and the carpet was once again clean and white.

It made sense in a strange sort of way. Her story about being trapped with an unkind boss and having no other place to go... and besides that, Brownie magic was something that no other Fae-folk could define. If the Dhrow were long-lived and the Elvhen damn near immortal, the Brownies were the great equalizers. They could move in and out of human or Fae territories without effort, block any and all magic for a long time, and they were the only Fae who could hide themselves from other Fae consistently. Of course, Iffear's head piercer was a Brownie.

The more he stayed in this town the more magical beings he became aware of. And that thought pulled him back to those damnable pixies and what they'd done...

Leaping to his feet, he ignored the indignant squeal from Mai and all but shoved Chinsie out of the way as he began to rip the blankets away to get to Iffear himself. The moment his chest was clear he ripped the dragon-stone from around his neck.

"Oh, for fuck's sake!" Mai's voice sounded disgusted as she just... appeared on the bed next to him. She cupped the stone carefully, hissing as it touched her skin. She pulled back to wave a white silk cloth into existence before surrounding the stone carefully and lifting it to her chest. "Poor baby," she crooned.

Vulwin stared at her for a moment, before dropping his gaze down to his lover. With the dragon-stone no longer touching Iffear's skin, Vulwin could now see huge black pustules forming where the stone had rested against his heart.

"Iffear," he whispered. "I -- I don't know what to do." With the absence of the stone, his lover didn't seem to be growing any stronger, and as he checked on their bond the yellow sickness was still there.

Whining under his breath, he reached out and ran his hands over his dragon's face and down to his chest. "I don't know what to do," he repeated, resting his forehead against Iffear's cool one. Never had he ever felt so weak and helpless before. Tears swam in his eyes as he tried to contemplate the loss of his mate, of his shining future. No. It wasn't right. It wasn't fair. Iffear had done nothing to deserve this fate and... and...

"Well, I do." Mai's voice broke through his self-pity and pulled his watery gaze to hers. "First, you stop crying and being defeatist. Are you a Dhrovish warrior or are you just another useless noble?"

That put some steel in his spine as he sat up and

stared at her. "What do you know, Brownie?"

"I can feel the mercury salts that cursed this poor soul."

"Mercury salts?" But how... but what..."

"Think of your elemental magic, prince. Yours is earthbound as a Dhrow and that means your innate magics will neutralize almost anything used against you. It is in the Dhrovish nature to protect itself until you are mature. You are years from true maturity, so mercury salts mixed with" -- she ran her hand over the silk-wrapped stone again --"Rowan. I am feeling rowan and yew. Yes, yew berries and roots, rowan branches and leaves, elements of earth, wind, water, and fire. All four combined and willingly accepted... Earth could accept fire and maybe wind, but the influx of water would have tipped this poison to the dangerous point for anyone except a Dhrow."

Chinsie curled up right on Iffear's chest as Mai mused more. Vulwin's mind was racing, going through tactics, tossing out theories and ideas...

"Me. This poison was used as a ruse to get to me. This would not have killed me, but if someone who was not a mature Dhrow, someone under my protection..."

"Someone poisoned him to make you suffer and it is clear that nothing but a miracle would kill you." Mai's words were blunt and matched what he was thinking.

"Why? I mean... we got this from drug-dealing pixies... but the pixies had to get it from somewhere..."

"Ponder it later." Vulwin blinked and Mai appeared across the room -- Brownie magic was a thing to behold -- and tucked the dragon-stone into a lined box that appeared out of thin air. "For now, you need to go and sing this baby to its final rest."

Hope filled Vulwin, and it was an amazing feeling. Mere moments ago, he was ready to curl up and offer his life, his death, his virility, anything to save his dragon, and then he discovered that his dragon loved him, *truly* loved him. And when he was about tumble into despair, a benevolent Brownie had given him hope once more. Iffear had gifted him with so much... so much. And now because of that, he had a chance to bring his beloved back to him.

"Wait until sundown?" he mused. "I don't think... he is so weak --"

"Chinsie's bond with Iffear has no connection to you, Dhrow," Mai instructed as he offered her a small smile. "It is pure and therefore sustaining and bolstering his life. This will not kill him, Vulwin Valas, Vulwin of the Silver Eye, Prince and next in line of the Shining Throne. This was designed to make you suffer. But that will not be happening. We'll sustain him, and you must prepare yourself. You assisted in the last singing, yes?"

"Yes." He nodded, rising from the bed and moving toward Mai.

"Then you know what must be done. But this will be harder. You are not a dragon and the only link you have to this stone is from Iffear himself. Meditate on that link, on your bond, and I will retrieve you when the time is right."

"Where? I have to get dressed and scout out an area --"

"The roof, Dhrovish prince." Mai seemed amused by the confusion on his face. "Remember Iffear keeps a rooftop garden. We grow the best herbs for magics and potions there... not to mention Chinsie's catnip and Iffear's weed."

And that made Vulwin snicker. His prim and proper dragon toking up on the roof? He had to see this.

"It's a sacred place protected by Brownie magic. This little one will find rest there. Your job is to prepare for the day's waning. We will take care of our dragon and you do the rest."

Nodding, Vulwin turned toward the bathroom and paused. "I -- I, uh --"

"Broke the glass to the shower? Didn't turn off the hot water? Left a prince-size mess in there with no servants to clean up after you?"

"I was desperate," Vulwin groused. "And I've never had a servant a day in my life. You confuse me with an Elvhen prince. I fix my own messes."

"True." Mai winked. "But just this one time, because you are stressed, I took care of it for you. Now go and bathe and meditate. I'll get you when the sun begins to die."

That said, she shooed him to the bathroom like he was a child, and Vulwin found himself amused. There was a Brownie in his bedroom with his injured mate and his familiar cat, one who was wearing designer jeans and a band T-shirt, with tattoos up and down her arms and the sharpest fangs he had ever beheld. Never would he ever have even thought that his life would turn out like this. Even in the midst of tragedy and plotting he was finding... joy in life.

With that thought in his head, he entered the now clean bathroom, crossed to the massive bath they never really used, and began to chant as he filled it with scalding water. He had to prepare to help heal that wounded lost soul... and then... then he was going hunting.

* * *

It seemed that he had been chanting for mere moments, holding onto that bond that connected him to his mate, cradling the blue thread, as he did his best to tighten the link between them. He could feel the green threads of Iffear's magic thicken and pulse back against the sickness that threaten to consume it. The protective magic deepened in color, though there were several gaps where the magic was doing its best to devour it whole. He could feel the love, and compassion, and joy, and passion of his mate, and that is what he held on to. He inserted his silver threads of magic where he could, using his own personal magic to shore up any weakening spots.

Their bond grew stronger under his nurturing, and he began to understand the complex magic that created the power of his dragon. And now as he opened his eyes, he could feel them pulse with the strength of their bond. He turned his head to see what had disturbed him and discovered Mai standing there. She looked a bit tired but more serious than he had ever seen her.

"It's time." Her voice was as determined as her expression as she held out a long white tunic to him.

Vulwin rose from water long grown cold and unnoticed and stretched his arms above his head, loosening muscles that hummed with the need for action. A wave of his hand dried him completely as he stepped from the tub. He reached for the knee-length tunic, tugging it over his head, then pulling his hair back over his shoulders. "On the roof," Mai intoned and Vulwin moved into the bedroom.

Iffear was again swaddled in blankets, but he didn't seem as pale as he had before. Chinsie was purring gently against his chest, and Iffear appeared to be at peace. With one final look at his mate, Vulwin turned to follow Mai to a stairwell near the elevator and up the stairs they concealed.

When he reached the top of the wide wooden steps, he had to pause and take it all in. Spread out before him was a lush lawn of vibrant green grasses, flowering plants, well-organized garden plots, and pots of the most beautiful blooms he had ever seen. The whole area was enclosed in a glass structure that let in the light but kept out the noise and pollution of the city below. It was a piece of paradise. It was the perfect place to lay a soul to rest.

Vulwin looked up and saw the sun just tipping below the skyline and knew it was time. Taking the box that Mai offered, he flipped open the lid and pulled out the silk-covered stone.

The feel of the corruption had lessened, and he turned to Mai for the reason. "I washed away the poison and the silk drew a lot of it away, neutralized it. I was able to extract a lot of it from Iffear, but when this precious little one is given peace, then he can truly begin to heal."

Nodding, Vulwin uncovered the amber stone, wincing as he felt the sobs of the unborn soul. Hefting it up by the chain, he held it up to the light of the dying day. It was beautiful, in a sinister yet enchanting way. He closely examined the swirl and color that lay inside, staring into a nearly golden abyss, and if he stared a little bit harder, he could almost make out a sliver of silver swimming in infinity, beating against its confines, screaming in agony.

Stepping back, he moved to the center of the garden, feeling the rich, living earth beneath his feet, feeling it enhancing his own magic with each step. When the magic made him stop, he noticed that he was at the north-facing side of the roof.

Once there, he dropped to his knees, pressed his forehead against the grass, and began to chant.

"Of the Five, The Fates, The Designers, hear me.

From the North, the strength of the earth, our strength, feel me."

Rising to his feet, he moved to the east side of the rooftop garden.

"Of the Five, The Fates, The Designers, hear me.

From the East, the strength of the wind, uplift me."

He moved to the south and repeated his actions.

"Of the Five, The Fates, The Designers, hear me.

From the South, the strength of fire, temper me."

He moved to the west, to where the sunset was exploding in vibrant color, and again dropped to his knees, pressing his forehead into the grass.

"Of the Five, The Fates, The Designers, hear me.

From the West, the strength of water, control me."

He moved to the north point again, bowing three times before carefully walking backward to the center of the circle he had created, stopping where magic bade him to do so.

"Of the Five, The Fates, The Designers, hear me.

From the Center, the source, the soul,

Master me, Break me, Bend me, Set me free to do your will.

I am your source, your fount, your conductor.

Through me, let your will be done."

As if it were a physical thing, Vulwin felt the magics rise up, felt them travel from the pure, sacred earth to flow up through his body in a rush so powerful it could be mistaken for ecstasy. In a wave so powerful, he was forced to his toes, his arms outstretched, his head tossed back, and his mouth opened as power he had never imagined flowed through him, compelling him, demanding of him.

He had no choice, no other recourse. He closed his eyes, the amulet dancing from his left hand, and he began to sing.

"Free! You are free. Never again will you feel this pain.

Your soul is free never again to feel fear.

Your soul is free, never again to experience anguish.

You are free! You are free! You are free!

Your life has been extinguished yet your soul carries on.

You existed for a purpose and though that purpose remains unknown.

Gone is the time of mourning what would be.

You are free. You are free. You are free.

You were wanted, you were loved. You were a cherished life.

You are now a being of perfection and light.

Never again feel the pain that this life forced upon you.

Never will you know of the pain life could carry for you.

Though your right to exist was stolen,

The sacred circle of life broken,

No more do you exist in misery.

You are Free. You are free. You are free."

When the very last note was ripped from his body, Vulwin collapsed facedown to the lush earth, waves of magic still ripping through him.

He stirred once, his cock swelling to its fullest before he exploded, tearing cries of ecstasy from his throat as he spilled his seed into the earth, an offering of seed and magic.

He rolled to his back, still panting as the stone in his hand began to vibrate. He rolled his head to the side to observe, and watched as the stone... shattered.

The amber stone shook, and with the tinkling sound of breaking crystal, the stone exploded into a million tiny shards that then turned in on themselves and exploded, leaving behind slivers of silver that evaporated until nothing remained but the barest sheen of magic.

From nowhere and from everywhere, a childish laugh filled the garden, a gleeful sort of sound that filled his heart with joy and pulled a smile from his tired lips. He watched as a sliver of silver-green rose up from the grass and swirled around him in joy and ecstasy, finally, only the Fates knew for how long, free.

He felt the light push of magic against his lips, against his eyes, and in his ear, he heard whispered one name.

Claddafin.

He had been given a name. Anger ignited within his chest, and with every breath, that anger blossomed into something more. Hatred filled Vulwin, hatred for what he had done, for what he had wrought, for what his very existence was forcing him to do next.

He had a name. His wrath had a target. The short-eared bastard would pay in blood and pain. He would joyously bathe in his entrails. Before his life could begin anew with his mate at his side, another's life must end. So be it. His prey would burn.

Dragon Heart (Dragon 3)
A Paranormal Women's Fiction Novella
Stephanie Burke

Vulwin and Iffear know who was responsible for the attempts on their lives and how these attacks were carried out; they now only need to discover why. Seeking revenge could shatter the tentative peace and reignite the war between two Fae factions but blood spilled in hate demands justice. How far will they go to fulfill a blood oath and see the Dragon Stones laid to rest once and for all?

Chapter One

"I will kill them all." Vulwin wasted no time in breaking the magic circle he had created and stumbling down the stairs to his Dragon.

Mai hustled after him, looking as incensed as a Brownie could look as she flicked her fingers at him, cleaning him up and changing his clothes into a longer black tunic as he moved.

Vulwin had several things on his mind at the moment, but first he wanted to be with his mate. He left the wooden stairs and made it to the bedroom where Chinsie still sat beside a slumbering Iffear.

"Well, the link is broken to the chain and the poison," Mai informed him as he moved into the bathroom. There was a popping sound and a smell of fresh herbs filled the air. "But you might want to bathe him to remove the rest. I have drawn a bath of elderberry, honeysuckle, plantain, and comfrey. It should soothe his pain and pull out what is left of the poisons in his system. I'm going to burn these sheets and change the bed... and then you can tell me what that grateful soul whispered to you."

"A name, Mai," Vulwin spoke softly as he unwound his Dragon from the blanket that encased him as Chinsie looked on. "It gave me a name."

Mai tilted her head to the side and considered her friend's mate for a moment. "I am to assume that this name will cease to be?"

"You can be assured that his direct line will cease to be," Vulwin growled, but the aggression was restricted to his voice as he tenderly cradled his Dragon in his arms. His eyes filled with love as he stared down at Iffear.

"Bathe." Mai waved her hand toward the

waiting bath. "Get out and take your romantic nonsense with you. I have work to do. Chinsie and I are going to ward this house properly now that my secret is out."

"Iffear didn't know?" Vulwin pulled his eyes away from his mate long enough to ask.

"He suspected, but then he left me to my privacy. He gave me a choice. He has always given me choices. He's cool like that."

"Yes, he is," Vulwin agreed before turning and exiting the room, his mate in arms, and he felt powerful Brownie magic begin to cleanse the air.

He had no idea how long he sat in the tub, cradling his mate close before Iffear jerked in his arms, his eyes snapping open.

"Settle," Vulwin purred at Iffear, hugging him tighter to his chest. "Settle, my Dragon."

"What happened?"

Vulwin smiled to discover not a hint of weakness in his mate's voice. He watched, amazed, as Iffear sat up, his eyes traveling around the room, before he turned and centered his gaze onto him. "Vulwin?"

"You were poisoned."

Iffear's eyes widened at that before a low growl rolled from his throat. "How?"

His hand went to his chest, going to grip the amulet, and he started when he discovered that there was nothing there. Again his gaze went to Vulwin for an explanation.

"I sang it to rest, my Dragon. The soul is at peace." Vulwin felt the tension leave his mate as he relaxed against him again.

"Yes." Iffear was nodding. "I don't feel its lure anymore, nor its cries of pain." He looked up at Vulwin, his red eyes glittering in joy. "I thank you, my mate."

"It was also how you were poisoned." Vulwin knew that his voice had deepened in anger, but he couldn't help himself. Someone had tried to make him suffer, to take away the one thing that he held most dear.

"It would not have killed me." Iffear sniffed. "I am virtually indestructible, even more so with your protections holding me safe." He waved the threat away. "It was a stupidity of their belief system and outdated information, I would assume."

"Yet they did this to annoy me? To claim my vengeance? To start a war? It doesn't make sense." Vulwin reached out and pulled his Dragon into his arms, inhaling his scent, feeling his body warm and alive in his arms. "Why?"

"Miscalculation, I suppose." Iffear hugged Vulwin back just as hard. "I am sorry I scared you."

"Having a mate passing out mid-coitus will do that to a Dhrow." Vulwin relented and joked a little, though he was still horrified at the thought of losing his mate. "You stole years of my life away."

Iffear snorted, flicking him on the nose with a wet finger. "You haven't even reached maturity yet, Dhrow. You have years to spare. And then you can't start losing them until after our son is grown. Seeing you have a neat piece of contraception jewelry, um... thrust upon you, that won't even happen until the king decides to release you."

Iffear chuckled but stopped as Vulwin stiffened in his arms. "Say that again?"

"No son, because you haven't reached your majority?" Iffear pulled back enough to look back up at him again. "Contraception ring?"

"It is not common knowledge that I have not yet

reached the age of my majority," Vulwin said carefully as his mind roared with plots and information and schemes. Being politically minded was a bitch some days, but in other ways it did more than make one suspicious of everyone else's motives. Sometimes it pointed you in the correct direction whether you wanted it to or not. "Yet everyone was aware that you were in heat."

"Of course." Iffear snarled a little. "They chained me up and paraded me before their figures and your guard. I damn near climbed you like a tree in the audience chamber, and I am quite sure everyone felt our bond solidify when you first took me, so I'd say yes. Everyone knew that I was in heat."

"Then everyone would expect you to be carrying now, wouldn't they?"

"I'd say yes, as no one knows about the nifty piece of jewelry your father gifted you with."

"Then they would know that my protections for any young that we created would not be fully established, correct?"

Iffear blinked as he sat back, amusement fleeing as anger began to turn his eyes a bright golden red. "This was an attack on my unborn child?"

"He would not even be established enough to become a Dragon Stone. He would have to be laid for that. But he would have been established enough to be recognized as my son... and his destruction would have meant that I would be cursed to a half-life, unable to hold my son or to deliver upon him the bulk of my love. I would have been shattered."

"They used me to get to you." Iffear's skin was starting to redden as scale imprints began to appear on his body. "They would murder my child to make you suffer? They would extinguish a life to be... petty? Tell me this name, Dhrow. I wish to know whose blood I will bathe in before the sun sets yet again."

"I think you are already acquainted with him, my love." Vulwin felt the coolness of waiting death settle over his body and mind. "Lord Claddafin the Bold."

"So Claddafin will not live to see another day," Iffear promised, rising from the water, smoke flowing from his nose.

"Not yet." Vulwin also rose to his feet, wrapping his arms around his lover, feeling his temper rise as his body began to shift. "Settle, my Dragon."

"Why the fuck not?" Iffear roared. "I will have my revenge, Dhrow, with or without you."

"You are a prince consort, Iffear," Vulwin reminded him as a wicked smile spread across his lips. "Now that we have proof, we can ruin him, end his life, force him to lose what standing he has amongst his people, make him a pauper and a complete outcast before we rend his body limb from limb."

Iffear was listening. He calmed and the scale pattern on his skin never fully erupted into scales, the precursor for a Dragon transformation. "And how would we do this?"

"Well..." Vulwin pressed a light kiss to his lips. "First, I'm going to write a letter to my father."

Chapter Two

From where he reclined naked in their bed, Kno stared at his lover as King Tartran crumpled the correspondence he held in his hand. The letter from the prince had arrived through channels meant for the most urgent news, and the king had wasted no time in retreating to his private quarters to read it. And now Tartran sat in his chair, black eyes blazing with unholy anger, dark earth magic sparkling from his form.

"What did the Silver have to say?" Kno asked, referring to the descriptor that was used to distinguish him from every other Vulwin in the realm. It was an homage to the powerful silver earth energy that resided in his body and the one silver eye he possessed, a legacy from his mother.

"Is your sword arm still steady?" Tartran asked as he rose to his feet. A flick of his fingers had the kingly embroidered tunic and pants he had donned for his evening's rest flashing away and his hardened battle leathers taking their place. "Have years at my side as my advisor and lover dulled your senses?"

A merciless grin spread across Kno's face as he climbed from the bed and an angry flash of red had him dressed in solid black leathers with the blazing red flame of a Holy Half-Dead burning from his chest. It was a warning to all who dared challenge him that he would not die, he would heal, and those who opposed him would perish painfully once they faced his wrath.

Unlike most Half-Dead who traveled the Fae realm in service to their king, Kno remained general and commander of one of Tartran's largest armies as well as advisor and lover to the king. The Dhrow was drenched in power and he wielded it as he should, as the right hand of the king and eventual left hand of the prince when the king felt the need to step down.

"Are we hunting?" Kno was always ready for a bloodletting. It was his bloodthirsty nature that made him a target in the Elvhish wars. Eagerly he called forth his sword, the silver blade dripping with the blood of redcaps and the juice of the rowan berries. He examined the poisonous thing before sheathing it in its scabbard and resting it low against his hips. "What are we hunting, or -- I hope -- who?"

The king, with his blade of cold ebony iron laced with rowan ash, offered his lover a small kiss on the lips before sheathing his own battle blade.

"You are going to love this." Tartran stepped back and waited for the explosion of eager magic which would flow from his lover's core. "We hunt Elvhen."

The king was not disappointed.

* * *

It was nearly sundown again when Vulwin felt his father's call. Walking to the kitchen, he stoppered the sink and filled it full of cold water. He tapped the porcelain sink three times and watched as a clear picture of his blood-soaked father appeared on the surface.

The king blinked once before speaking. "This scrying bowl, Vulwin. It is very precise and clear."

"It's a porcelain sink," Vulwin explained. "It's a stone compound made of the earth."

"So much better than silver." His father nodded. "I must have some."

"I will personally bring several to you if you have found my quarry. Have you, Father? Have you discovered where the foul serpent ran to ground?"

"I have narrowed your search, and I have an audience with their king." Tartran's grin was the stuff of nightmares. Vulwin had never seen it outside of a battle or when dealing with idiot nobles that were solidly wrong and in danger of a beheading. It was almost frightening to see the staid and proper king so eager for bloodshed. Well, Vulwin thought, it was something he and his father had in common.

"Where?"

"Several little snakelings have pointed him toward the south and the Wyldlands. I am given to understand that the copse of the King of Trees is infected. With your skills and knowledge, I am sure that you can wrangle one small snake and deliver it unto me at the Elvhen Court, my son."

"Your will shall be eagerly done, Your Shining Majesty." Vulwin might not notice it, but his evil smile perfectly matched that of his father's.

"One more thing."

Vulwin turned his attention back to his father when he spoke. "I will require the injured party to travel with me to appear at the Court of King Ovorion Nallos, The, uh… Great."

"For political reasons?" he asked, trying to think through his father's strategies.

"No," the king growled. "For sheer intimidation. Those short-eared bastards deserve to stew in their own fear. They allowed one of their own to perpetuate this disgusting chokehold on the very creatures we are now aligned with… in blood. In short, we are connected in a way to the Dragonish people that they could never imagine would happen because of the actions of one of theirs. They allowed one of their own to harm our people. I want them staring down the throat of a probable war fought on two fronts, two *united* fronts. I want those bastards pissing their breeches, and I want them to know that their fate lies in the hands of those they thought to subjugate. Even if the king has no knowledge of what one of his high lords was doing, he had to have felt the abuse of the magic in those cursed Dragon Stones and chose to ignore it. I see it is time we make him regret those poor decisions, my son. I want your mate to make him regret those decisions."

Vulwin looked over his shoulder at Iffear, who had followed him into the kitchen and grinned when he smiled, his normal blunt human teeth replaced with a set of sharp, layered fangs that made Mai's look like milk teeth.

"Your will be done," Vulwin agreed and watched as Iffear turned and exited the kitchen. He bowed to his father and drained the water.

"Iffear," he called, following his lover into the bedroom. His Dragon was opening up closets and pulling down a chest filled with nothing but shimmering jewel-encrusted chains. "Oh," he gasped as Iffear hefted what had to be several pounds of precious metals, watching as the light passed through the stones that studded almost every link.

"Formalwear." He grinned as he transferred several handfuls of chains into a silk-lined leather bag.

"Dragons have formalwear?" he questioned, moving to embrace his lover from behind. "What do you wear that over?"

"That is all the formalwear." Iffear chuckled as Vulwin's cock instantly hardened while he pictured his lover wearing nothing but these fine jewels and metal chains.

"You are going to run around naked in the presence of two kings?" Vulwin purred. "The people will see the perfection of your body but dare not touch for you are chosen, marked and claimed by me. I think that is turning me on."

"Every fucking thing turns you on since you lost your contraception ring," Iffear teased back before turning in his lover's arms to press up against his body. "Now how about marking me up before I take my leave. I wouldn't want them to think that I'm being neglected..."

Vulwin attacked, taking his lips in a powerful hiss, pushing him back against the closet and pressing his taller, thinner form against that of his mate's.

"You want to be marked?" Vulwin growled, dipping his head to lap at his Dragon's neck, over the mating bite that had scarred so beautifully perfect. "I can do that. Gonna mark every inch of this flesh so that they all know that you are mine."

A wave of his magic had Iffear pinned and lifted against the closet doors, his perfect body on display and immobile at his command. The backlash of excited pleasure from their bond made Vulwin's cock so hard it began to ache even while his heart raced. All that power, all that majesty, all that was beautiful was his Dragon... and it was all under his control.

Iffear moaned as he slid up the doors and Vulwin guided his legs over his shoulders, stopping when his mate's cock was at the level of his mouth.

Iffear had a pretty cock. It was long and thick and the scaled pattern under the soft skin felt so good when it was reaming his ass properly. Now he had a chance to get a closer look and relished the moans his mate released when he gripped him gently in one hand and let the other explore.

"Vulwin, *fuck*..." Iffear groaned, his head thumping back against the doors as he relaxed in his mate's magical grip. His body began to quiver slightly and his skin heated under Vulwin's touch.

"Eventually," Vulwin purred at his mate as he ran gentle fingers over the deep red head of Iffear's cock and tightened his grip on the thick shaft.

"Fucker --"

"Relax." Vulwin chuckled. "I'll get you there. For now, I want to play with what is mine." He leaned forward and blew a stream of cool air over Iffear's cock before he sucked the spade-shaped head deeply into his mouth.

"Vulwin!" his mate hissed as Vulwin extended a little extra magic to hold him in place. Iffear was straining against his hold, his muscles bulging as they fought against the magical restraints that held him, for the most part, immobile and spread wide for his pleasure.

"So beautiful, baby." Vulwin pulled off his mate's cock long enough to praise him before he began to suck him in deeply. He moaned as he ran his tongue over the scales' imprints, feeling them harden as he began to drool over the flavor of his mate. Iffear tasted of earth and fire, of growing things and of the tantalizing remains of his heat, still lingering in his blood. His Dragon's cock was a tasty diversion, but his beautiful dick was not the only thing on offer.

He released the shaft and allowed his fingers to dance lower over his wet vaginal opening that was soft and hot and slick...

Without warning he thrust three fingers in and smiled around his mouthful of cock as his mate howled in pleasure. Iffear began to thrash, his head turning from side to side as he shrugged to no avail to free his hands. He trembled, his temperature rising again, his body flushing red with the buildup of pleasure, and Vulwin wanted more. He wanted his Iffear screaming and creaming on his fingers before he fucked him through the damn closet door.

"Fuck, *harder!*" Iffear whined as he writhed against the wall, the magic holding him, against his mate's touch. Through their bond, Vulwin could feel his mate's desperation as Iffear's muscles tightened while his body was denied the orgasm it craved. Still Vulwin fucked him with his fingers, twisting them in his silken heat, touching upon nerves that made Iffear scream as smoke began to flow from his nose and mouth.

"Oh, this is perfect," Vulwin purred. "I am sure those short-eared bastards are going to drool over you, imagine doing this to you, imagine fucking you against any flat surface they can find or conjure. And they can't. Do you know why?"

Iffear shook his head as Vulwin grabbed his cock once more and began to pump it in time with the thrusts from his fingers where they danced inside his body.

"Do you know why?" Vulwin roared, leaning over to lap at the now leaking head of Iffear's dick, sucking down his precum like it was the most delicious thing he had ever had the pleasure of savoring before sucking him down his throat, swelling around him while his mate hissed and thrashed beneath him.

"B-because I belong to you!" Iffear finally forced out. Vulwin decided to reward him for his answer.

He dropped his Iffear's cock from his mouth and tore his fingers from his body before a wave of his hand sent his mate soaring across the room to spin and land flat on his back.

"If you don't fuck me --" Iffear tried to move, and the moment he realized he couldn't because he was still trapped in his mate's magical web was something that Vulwin would never forget. The

Dragon's bright red eyes widened, then narrowed as he glared at him. Then he relaxed into the bindings, letting his body go limp as he began to purr.

"Oh, fuck." Vulwin had a moment to regret his humor at the situation before Iffear began to deftly send waves of lust and desire down their bond straight to his groin.

The sudden slam of pleasure nearly brought Vulwin to his knees. His cock, already hard and throbbing from the taste of his mate, the feel of his slick on his fingers, seemed to grow impossibly harder, and his spine stiffened as waves of lust flowed through his body.

He stumbled toward the bed, toward his Dragon, and growled as he fell on top of him.

"Fucking tease," Vulwin complained as Iffear let out a low laugh.

"Come fuck me, Vulwin, my mate," he urged. "Send me to them smelling like you just let me out of your bed, the marks of your ownership shining brightly through my gold. Come fuck me, mate. Give me all that you have so that I may carry you into battle with me."

There was no stopping him after that.

Vulwin dropped his magical bindings, and in an instant Iffear rolled over and pounced.

It was good thing the bed was so large because two fully grown males falling into rut took up a lot of space.

Vulwin was biting at Iffear, sinking his fangs into every inch of skin he could, leaving little red marks to be licked and sucked until they were bruises.

Iffear was no better, scratching and purring, biting at Vulwin's long neck, trying to mark his territory between the spread of silver stars that marked

Vulwin's black skin. Sweat poured from their bodies, and the sounds they were pulling from each other were loud and unapologetic. If they had neighbors, they would have known both of their names, they got so loud in their fucking.

"This is my ass," Vulwin roared, gripping Iffear's rounded cheeks as he flipped his mate onto his stomach before leaning down and taking a big bite, leaving behind his teeth marks in a spectacular bruising imprint. "It's perfect and it's mine."

Iffear howled in agreement, rising up to his knees to present his ass for more painful pleasure, to present the perfect target for his mate's lustful wrath.

"This cock is mine too," Vulwin went on, pulling his lover's hard, leaking cock straight down and stroking it harshly before dropping to his back to slide between his mate's thick thighs and suck it into his mouth once more, nursing on it before he delivered a hard smack to Iffear's left cheek, the one without the bite mark.

Iffear moaned in agreement, arching his hips higher, and his hands began to tear at the furs that covered the bed. He spread his legs wider and began to thrust straight down into Vulwin's throat, fucking his face madly as Vulwin began to deliver a series of hard smacks to Iffear's perfect ass.

After a moment, he grabbed two handfuls of his rounded cheeks and began to knead Iffear's flesh, spreading him wider with each caress before he let his fingers trail over his opening down to his sopping wet hole. He sank three fingers in and held on as Iffear began to slam back onto his fingers before fucking down in his throat.

It was a wild, disjointed rhythm, but it was doing it for Iffear because he was gasping, begging, crying for

Vulwin to fuck him properly.

"Who am I to not give my mate all that he desires?" Vulwin pulled off to purr before he rolled onto his back, tugging Iffear until he got the idea and straddled his hips.

Vulwin growled as Iffear reached back and grabbed his dick, giving it a few hard strokes, spreading his leaking precum around. He positioned himself at Iffear's opening and Iffear sank down with a yowl.

"Fuck," Vulwin growled, his hands going to his mate's hips, his grip tight enough to leave bruises as he placed his feet flat to the bed for leverage and thrust his hips up as hard as he could.

Iffear showed his appreciation by bending over and clamping his teeth onto Vulwin's neck.

"Fuck yes, mark me back," Vulwin purred as he and Iffear dropped into a rapid rhythm that soon began to consume the both of them.

Vulwin could feel his dick trapped in his mate's warm, wet heat, felt his silken muscles tighten every time Iffear slammed down, and reluctantly loosen as he pulled up. He opened his eyes to see his mate's head thrown back, eyes closed as he grunted and growled with his movements, white smoke pouring from his body as he gave in to the pleasure that was flowing through him, that was flooding their bond with delight, that was turning him into a gasping, greedy creature that couldn't ride his mate's cock hard enough.

Vulwin fought to hold on, to not just give in and explode into his release no matter how hard Iffear was pulling it from him. His heart was racing, his body going into spasms, his balls pulling up against the base of his cock as his mate rode him hard and with beautiful abandon.

"Iffear," he panted, tossing his head to knock the tendrils of his white hair from his face. "Fuck, my mate... What you do to me..."

He whined and slammed his eyes closed as fire danced up his spine, tightened his stomach and his thighs. He had to close his eyes for a moment to gain control... and then his Dragon began to purr.

The vibrations from Iffear's body traveled straight to his cock, making it even harder as his mate tried to strangle it with his body. This was new and it threw him off rhythm as his head snapped back and his hips lost his thrust, the one that let him just slam up into Iffear as hard as he could.

"Fuck, Dragon," he shouted before he got a grip on his body and spun them on the bed once more, Iffear on the bottom, his legs up around his ears as Vulwin damn near bent him in two.

"Yes!" Iffear wailed. "Yes! Fuck me!"

His Dragon's body was flushing red, scale patterns were pushing their way up through his skin; his mouth was open and white smoke poured from his lips, making the air around him hot and steamy. HIs Dragon was on fire, and it was up to him to quench the flames.

He fucked his Dragon harder, grinding his cock in deep at the end of each thrust, pulling out slowly only to slam in again harder as his Iffear stiffened beneath him.

"Yes," Vulwin urged him. "Yes, come on, my Dragon. Come on. Feel me. Feel me fucking you like you like. Take it, mate. Take all of me."

Iffear was beyond words, his body growing taut as their bond fairly screamed in pleasure. He was sobbing, his heart racing, his eyes closed as he gave into the ecstasy Vulwin was bringing him.

"Come on," Vulwin urged again, reaching for Iffear's cock and managing to give it a good stroke before Iffear threw back his head and screamed.

"Fuck, yes," Vulwin groaned as he felt his mate's body ripple around his dick. He fucked into him again and again, riding Iffear's orgasm, extending it, ramping up the pleasure as he served his mate's desire.

The sight of Iffear, his body slamming up against his own, his perfect cock shooting his seed over Vulwin's hands in slick stripes over his chest and up his face, the way he moaned his name as he sank back onto the bed furs...

It was too much. Vulwin felt his cock swell to its fullest and his balls churn as he began to shoot deep within his mate.

"Fuck, Iffear!" he roared as his mind went white, as his hips slammed uncontrollably and without rhythm into his Dragon, as he felt Iffear's claws tear fire down his back, but the hot pain only added to the pleasure that was pulling him into a realm he had never experienced before.

He loved his mate. He desired his body. He wanted his heart bound to him as tightly as the Dragon's soul already was. He fucking loved his mate.

As his body gave one final shudder, he dropped onto Iffear's chest, lapping at a bit of skin that was nearest to his mouth as he needed to taste his mate to make the whole experience complete.

He was still purring as a laughing Iffear rolled him off of his body and snuggled up beside him.

"That was fun." Iffear's beloved voice almost an intrusion on the moment, but reality waited for no Fae, and Vulwin knew what they had to face.

But still, he got one more kiss in before his mate

began to move, before they both had to face the trials and tribulations that were sure to come as they finally took action against those who would oppress and malign them.

Revenge was at hand. It was nearly time.

Chapter Three

"I am definitely marked." His skin still tingling with the touch of his mate, Iffear stepped back from the bed and waved the massive skylight above it open.

"No shower?" Vulwin, who was still flat on his back struggling to breathe, asked.

"Hell no." Iffear knew his voice was dropping into a growl and grinned as his lover's sated cock lurched in a useless attempt to rise again. He had drained his Dhrow dry and still his lover wanted more. His feelings for the male reclining in his bed doubled over again. "I am going freshly fucked and marked by your hand. All will know that I have been claimed and have done the claiming in return. If they don't like it, they can be the first to line up and kiss my ass. The short-ears have a lot to answer for, and if my intimidating them on behalf of the long-ears --"

"Hey!" Vulwin protested, wiggling his own bejeweled, arching ears, "That's not the only thing long on me --"

"Then," Iffear went on, shaking his head at his adorable mate, "all the better. They will pay for what they have done, and they will pay in blood and in flame."

As he spoke, Iffear arched his back, closing his eyes as he let the control of his guise fall away.

He felt his skin bubble as the muscles underneath shifted. The raised scale patterns pressed through his skin, stealing the human tan and replacing it with a wave of emerald green and black. Along his head and back, bright red spikes rose and pressed through his skin and began creating the distinctive jeweled red mane that Dragons were prized for.

He shifted from foot to foot as his spine pushed

through his lower back, and a bright scarlet, spaded tail began to emerge. He arched into the change as the flesh on his sides parted and brilliant red wings began to emerge.

Iffear opened his eyes and stared down at his mate, noting his interest and taking note that there was no fear there at all. Vulwin had risen to his knees eagerly awaiting the rest of his change, but there was no room for that in his house.

"Chinsie," he called out as his neck began to elongate.

Carrying the silk-lined sack that contained his formalwear in her mouth, Chinsie leapt to his already changing head. He looked back at Vulwin, who seemed shorter and shorter as his body began to change. "I must fly. I will complete this change in the air. I will see you soon, my love," he crooned as his wings fully extended and he began moving them slowly, his metamorphosing body lifting in the air. "Good, safe hunting. Just because you cannot die doesn't mean you can't lose a limb."

"To those idiots?" Vulwin's voice was breathless as Iffear began to levitate toward the skylight. "Never."

"Then show them who you are, my mate. And I will make them remember what I can be."

"Show them hell," Vulwin purred, his cock hard and his eyes admiring as they ran over the Dragon's changing body. "Make them long for the void."

"With pleasure," Iffear assured him, then in a flash of green magic, he soared through the skylight, invisible to all but those with magical sight. His triumphant scream was masked in the sound of a ship's horn. Then he was in full Dragon form, flying to one of the many access points in the city that would take him back to the Fae.

He was going to put the fear of the Dragonish in those fucking elves. Never again would they forget what the Dragonish were, what they were capable of, Dragon Stones or not.

* * *

The Wyldlands were just as dark and quiet as he remembered, but thankfully he didn't have to search too hard to find a particular snake. Vulwin remembered his parting gift to the Elvhen Lord and that enabled him to track the bastard with ease.

The tiny shards of metal that had once made up the chains that bound his Dragon, the very chains that Vulwin imbued with his magic and exploded in the short-ear's face, would not have been able to be removed by any magical means. They were a lesson allowed by the Fates and eventually would have dissolved in his body and passed through his system, the scars a slight reminder to behave. Now those very same shards were leading him right to the bastard, the feel of his own magic unmistakable.

Now dressed in his familiar black armor, he deftly climbed the branches of Father Oak, invisible to those below, and watched as they roamed their camp set up in the neutral Wyldlands.

"Another week or so should do it," Lord Claddafin said to one of his guards, and if Vulwin wasn't mistaken, it was the very same guard that Chinsie had taken a chunk out of for injuring Iffear. "Then we will hear the mourning bells toll for the precious Silver Prince, just found a mate and now cursed to a half-life."

There was no amusement in his eyes, just anger and the thirst for revenge.

"But did you have to kill the Dragon?" the warrior muttered. "We could have reclaimed him.

There is no telling what a tamed Dragon is worth."

"You think he will be tamed?" Lord Claddafin motioned for his warrior to take a seat beside him at the camp table they'd set up. It was clear that they had established themselves here for a while; lavish tents had been set up, animals were roasting over three fires, provisions laid out neatly and ready for easy access. It was nice, as far as long-term camping went, which meant that they had been planning this for some time.

He poured his warrior a glass of wine and settled in to tell a story, and Vulwin settled into the arms of a tree to learn more about his enemy.

"A Dragon is never tamed by the loss of an egg. The beasts go mad with anger. They drop any guise of being Fae-kind and revert to their natural state, a dangerous, mindless beast."

"But they never live outside of war." The warrior picked up his wine and sipped. "Isn't that why the Dragon Stones work so well?"

"They are merely trying to reclaim something they consider their possessions. Any other being would mourn the loss and move on. It's not like it's really a life in the first place. It's just an egg, but that egg holds the spark of suggestion, of what it could be. That is enough to mark it as a possession, and Dragons are selfish, hoarding beasts who ape the part of us greater Fae."

"So it will go mad, and the Silver Prince will be stuck with a mindless beast for a mate." The warrior nodded. "It seems fair for what he cost you."

"No. The prince will more than likely use his bond to corral the beast, more's the pity. Those Pixies should have sold him the amulet by now. We know that he was in heat, so conception is assured. Dhrow --" He snorted. "Depraved monsters who will mate with anything. The bastards always breed true, and there will never be an end to them. Maybe this particular Dragon will blame the prince for his loss and turn against him and his line. Unlikely, but one can hope," Claddafin drawled on, drinking deeply from his own deep chalice of wine. "I just want the bastard to suffer. Vulwin scared me."

Claddafin ran his fingers over the small slivers of metal embedded in his cheeks. "He embarrassed me before that wretched king of his, and he murdered my son, my youngest, and the only one of my direct line to want to continue the family vows to avenge our line for the deaths of so many at the hands of those beasts in the Dragon Wars."

"Your son -- excuse me, my lord, for saying -- did kill a Dhrow first."

"And I blame myself for that." Claddafin sighed, taking another drink. "We have to be careful about how we use the stones. We only have a limited supply left as they were supposed to have been turned over to the Dragon lords at the completion of the peace pact. I wouldn't have let such an impulsive youngling get his hands on one, except he managed unsupervised use. He was too brash. Maybe if I had given him one --"

"Then King Ovorion would have known you still possessed them, and that would be going against royal decree. He would have to execute you to prevent another war with the Dragons."

"True." The lord nodded. "Yet I find it cold comfort when all I have left is the shredded remains of my youngest. One way or another, that pain must be answered for." Claddafin sniffed and took another drink. "They took his ears, Yousent, and they kept his beautiful perfect ears... those monsters."

Vulwin rolled his eyes at the display. Maybe if

the bastard had chosen not to break the law or reared his youngling to be a decent being, none of this would have happened. Vulwin had heard enough of the sob story. He was here to complete a job by order of his king. That meant he couldn't send an arrow through the bastard's eye. The one named Yousent, however...

There was a dull *thunk* and a look of shock and horror on Yousent's face before his left eye exploded in a glutinous mass of red and green. Vulwin made sure he saw his death coming before he changed positions, dancing in the arms of Father Oak while he pulled another arrow from his quiver.

"We are under attack!" the lord bellowed, leaping to his feet, knocking red wine and the bloodied remains of Yousent to the thick, dark grass.

Half of his remaining warriors raced out of the tents, pulling their lord toward the safety of the tents as they called out to their comrades in arms. No more came running from the forest because Vulwin had put down three fucking elves like the lowly, rabid animals they were while he'd hunted for this camp. Now he was just ready to have fun ridding himself of the ignorance of the others before he dragged the snake back before their king to answer for his crimes.

As silent as a wraith, Vulwin danced through the trees, firing deadly arrows at the panicking Elvhen warriors. They were equipped for a direct attack, not subterfuge from the shadows. Swords meant nothing when you couldn't find an enemy to rush and impale.

"There goes a toe!" he called out as one of the remaining three warriors took an arrow to the foot. The Elvhen trash screamed as the warhead of the arrow secured his foot to the ground, and his flesh started smoking from the yew wood the shaft was made from. If he managed to break the arrow to pull his foot free, he would have to deal with the iron shavings that packed the hollow shaft of the war arrow. Vulwin wasn't playing games. He wanted them to suffer.

"How many of them are there?" Lord Claddafin screamed as an arrow slammed into his buckler -- the small, round shield he kept at his side. He only then remembered he owned it and lifted it to provide some protection. The arrow hissed as it hit the enchanted silver of his shield, the poison in the war arrow dissolving the metal. "Find them!"

Vulwin made no effort to disguise his laughter at this point. One short-ear was down, and one was doing his best to lead Claddafin into one of the tents. Every time they took a step in that direction, however, Vulwin let loose a volley of arrows that prevented their retreat. If they even touched the ground where the arrow had pierced, their skin would start to slowly melt away.

One warrior rushed the trees, and in a disgustingly petty mood, Vulwin dropped down to sit on a branch before flipping backward. Holding on by his legs, he sighted the rushing warrior upside down and let an arrow fly, striking him in the throat. The warrior didn't have time to scream. He just dropped dead.

Giving up his game, Vulwin dropped to his feet and left the shadows of the trees, sure to place himself right in front of Claddafin and his one remaining guard.

"You!" Claddafin hissed, and Vulwin offered him a sarcastic bow.

"Me." He chuckled darkly. "I got tired of listening to your villainous monologue... though I guess it isn't a monologue if you were yapping at poor Yousent. It was a mercy killing for me to take him out, you know, and I am running an errand for my king. It seems your presence is wanted back in the Elvhen Court, Lord Claddafin. Did you not receive your invitation?"

With his bow in one hand and an arrow in the other, his black cloak waving with his barely leashed power, Vulwin stepped forth like death himself, dark and deadly. To those watching it appeared that the shadows lovingly caressed his body, reluctant to let him part from them. His eyes, one menacing black and the other a piercing silver, stared deeply into Claddafin's, who swore he could feel them boring into his soul.

"I am not going anywhere with you," Claddafin managed to stammer in a bluff. Was this the last thing his youngling had seen, Vulwin's dark visage and body that shouted of death, reaching out for him?

"Oh, I disagree. And if you don't want your remaining *warrior*" -- he sneered the word --"meeting the same fate as good old Yousent, I suggest you order him to stand the fuck down."

"To the void with you!" the warrior shouted, and then stepped around Claddafin to launch himself at Vulwin.

"For fate's sake," the archer spat before hefting his arrow and stepping forward to meet the charge.

He easily ducked a wild sword swing and spun around the warrior, his cloak flowing behind him like a living, breathing thing. It seemed to envelop the warrior for a second, and when he spun swiftly on his heel to strike out at the large being behind him, Vulwin simply used his arrow as a dagger and slammed it deeply into the warrior's right eye. He dropped as if all his strings had been cut, his battle cry -- his lord's name -- abruptly cut off.

Now Vulwin turned and smiled at Claddafin, stepping over the corpse of his fallen warrior. "Just you and me now," he spoke softly as Lord Claddafin began to panic.

"I am your better --"

"Clearly" -- Vulwin waved round at the arrow ridden camp and the bodies of the fallen --"Not."

A sly look settled on Claddafin's face before he opened his mouth to speak again.

"How's your mate?" he asked, his eyes scanning the area wildly for an exit.

"Why don't you ask him yourself?"

Claddafin's eyes grew wide while he searched the shadows for a suddenly rampaging Dragon. By the time he returned his gaze to Vulwin, the archer was standing right before him.

"You can't --"

"The hell I can't," he snarled before he let his fist fly, giggling to himself as he felt the delicate bones of the long Elvhish nose snap under his knuckles. "And they only said I had to bring you in. They didn't say what condition you had to be in other than alive."

What followed was the most pitiful yet oddly satisfying ass-whooping he had ever delivered to someone.

Hours later, Vulwin strode through the walls of the Elvhen Court, dragging a bloody, whimpering lord behind him.

Chapter Four

The shock on the faces of the Elvhish watching was a balm to Vulwin's soul, and he lifted his foot and kicked Lord Claddafin to land before the Elvhish King who sat emotionless on his throne. Then with all due pomp and circumstance, he bowed deep and low before his father.

"My Liege," he intoned deeply, ignoring the gasps of outrage by the watching Elvhish nobles, peering up at Tartran through a long fall of hair.

"My Prince," his father answered, nodding and giving him agency to stand before him. He took his place at his father's side, ignoring Kno's visible amusement at his actions.

"This behavior is beyond what is decent." A highly placed noblewoman, from her position next to the throne, tried to scold him. "He is king --"

"Not my king," Vulwin interrupted her, looking around the room filled with short-ears, surrounded by their magics and their bright colors. It was a pageant of hues and shades, and it was giving him a headache. "Where is Iffear?" he asked, needed to set eyes on his mate.

Snickering, Kno pointed upward and there, sitting amongst the rafters was the largest green-and-black-scaled Dragon he was sure the Elvhen had ever seen. He was quite sure his mate had given even his own father a shock when he flew through one of the natural portals that led to their realm.

He smiled as the Dragon took to wing, causing several of the nobles to titter in fear as he circled the wide golden audience chamber two times before descending to land with a crash in front of Vulwin.

"My Dragon," he purred as the massive beast

lowered its head to sniff at him. He was amazed at Iffear's sheer size, as he had not seen him fully transformed before he took to wing back in their human abode. Now at full height, Iffear stood at least three times Vulwin's. His bright red eyes were the size of Vulwin's head, at least, and a gorgeous set of scarlet jewels created the mane that trailed from the top of his head and flowed down to a thick, spaded tail. His horns were massive, spanning at least six feet on each side of his head, and the black-and-green scales created a flowing wave pattern over his whole body. His muzzle was solid black with green highlights along his cheekbones and around his eyes, and his horns and the long talons that graced each foot were a deep sharp onyx that were only slightly more terrifying than his rows of sharp, bright white teeth. He was a monstrous, beautiful, bejeweled thing, and Vulwin understood why generations ago his people had made a pact with the Dragon-folk to stay out of the Dragon Wars. He could picture an army of Iffears burning shit to the ground and shuddered because he could find no mental strategy to survive it.

Dragons were elemental, wild magic combined at its best and worst. If you garnered the ire of a Dragon, your best bet was to make amends right away and hope it didn't bring its brethren in to reap vengeance. From a small, strategic standpoint, Vulwin understood why the Elvhish would be driven to create such a thing as a Dragon stone to defend themselves. Yet a bigger part of him understood that even fear of a thing should not have been enough to make one pervert natural magic and steal lives in such a manner. Every method of control eventually broke, every cage had a door, and every perfect plan had a flaw. He understood the Dragons' rage when they were finally free and turned on their oppressors. No matter the worth of Dragon scales and their jeweled manes, you would have to be a damn fool to try and murder them for the bloody harvest.

Unafraid, he reached up and ran his fingers over the scarlet jeweled scales that ran over the ridges of his eyes. "Hello, my Dragon. Did you miss me? Did you have fun terrorizing these fools?"

Iffear reared back, opened his mouth, spread out massive scarlet wings, and let out a wailing shrill that vibrated the glass in the room and caused more than a few nobles to scream in shock at the long-remembered sound. The battle cry of a Dragon could vibrate bones and shatter glass, and shred eardrums if it so wished. Vulwin watched, arms crossed and nodding as if he understood some secret Dragon language as he checked on the bond between them. The threads were thick and powerful, twining together beautifully, the blue of true love pulsing wildly.

Iffear's abrupt change into human form nearly went unnoticed, so hard he was concentrating on their beautiful bond. He blinked once, and then standing before him, red eyes narrowed in anger, was Iffear's familiar human form, naked save for the jewels that encircled and draped thickly around his body.

Iffear moved forward and the links of gold and platinum shifted, exposing teasing glimpses of his tanned skin. His cock was shielded behind an elaborate jeweled knot while the rest of the links alternately exposed and teased with flashes of his perfect muscular flesh as he moved. He glittered like a hoard of jewels and this magnificent creature was all his.

"Very nice, mate," Vulwin purred, reaching out and cupping Iffear's cheek, drawing him in for a slow, deep press of lips and tongue. "Formalwear, you say?"

he asked as he pulled away, licking the taste his lover from his lips, savoring it as he once again allowed his gaze to roam over his perfect body.

"As formal as it gets." Iffear's deep voice shocked some of the watching Elvhen, though the king remained passive on his throne, his queen sitting nervously beside him. "And I see you brought in fresh meat... How very thoughtful of you, mate. I was feeling quite peckish."

Iffear turned to the whimpering lord on the floor, and a low rumbling growl filled the chamber.

"You can't have a snack now," Vulwin teased. "His blood would muss your beautiful outfit." He ran a hand tentatively over the links and held in his gasp of awe as he felt the power in the magic of the thing. It seemed each of the many jewels that dotted the chains were miniature focus points. They drew in his elemental magic, enhanced it, and made his mate all the more powerful without him actively drawing in magic with a spell or a chant. It was ingenious, and he couldn't think of any other creature who could have created it without burning out their core with the amount of magic the jewels were generating. It also would have lain dormant until Iffear placed this armor on his body, because no matter how pretty and delicate it looked, it was some serious armor. If this was formal, he wondered what the set of links for battle was like. He was alternately delighted and horrified at the thought.

"He is but one bite and would no doubt leave me feeling ill," Iffear sneered, turning his nose up at the bleeding Claddafin and instead turning to face Vulwin's father. "My king," he purred, and the watching Elvhen blanched and hissed, all the politically minded knowing how powerful those two words were. There was an alliance between the Dragons and the Dhrovish, and an attack on one was an attack on the other. This was something that had never occurred before in any of their extended lives.

"Prince Iffear," Tartran answered and even the venerable Kno offered him a bow. "Did you have fun terrorizing the villages and towns?"

"Not my fault if the flight of a Dragon creates such a horrible ruckus," Iffear answered sweetly, blinking innocently up at Vulwin's father... who didn't even bother to hide his snort of amusement.

"And now, my people are probably beating a path to my door," the Elvhish king finally spoke, his smooth tenor a balm on the ragged nerves of his people. "I trust you didn't set anything alight, Prince Iffear?"

The Elvhish king was the epitome of what it meant to be Elvhish; therefore, Vulwin despised him on sight. He was tall and slim, with golden hair that fell to his knees in waves. His skin was as pale as the moon, yet rusty and warm-appearing to the eye. He was dressed in thick white hose, a white and gold doublet covered his body to the upper thigh, and white fur boots encased his feet and legs to the knee. They were tied in place with jeweled chains, and he wore rings on every finger -- diamonds, no less, while his short, delicately pointed ears were pierced with several large stones of the same kind.

Iffear thought he looked like a useless popinjay.

Beside him sat his nervous wife, also as pale-skinned as he but with bright red hair that flowed nearly to her feet. She was dressed much as he, but her fur-trimmed white silk gown covered her completely from shoulders to feet. Around her neck was a massive necklace that nearly rivaled Iffear's chain outfit for sheer number of bejeweled chains. It started as a multicolored choker and flowed down to loop and wrap around her whole body. She wore rubies on her fingers and several silvery bangles around her wrists. Iffear smiled at her, and she paled further, leaning back against her husband as if seeking his protection.

"If I sent Dragon-flame out amongst your people, have no fear that you would not know." There was no respect in Iffear's words, and the king nodded, taking no offense at the tone.

"If what you say is true, then I understand your righteous anger, Prince Iffear. Nevertheless, you and your mate are as welcome in my hall as your king." He nodded to Tartran.

"Which means not at all, am I correct?" Iffear asked, then grinned at the Elvhish king who snorted in amusement. "My mate has been teaching me of Fae politics, and I must say that your kind make everything more complicated than it has to be. The Dragonish tell no lies, are open and direct, and we mean what we say."

"I suppose that would save time." The Elvhen king was amused. "Yet that is not our way, and not nearly as much fun."

"More's the pity," Iffear respond before the Dhrovish king began to speak.

"No, your way is to deflect the truth, to hide it in lies. Which is why I am here today, Ovorion."

"And you accuse another sitting king of such atrocities?" King Ovorion Nallos the Great asked, lifting one golden eyebrow. "Tartran, I thought you knew me better than that. I revel in truth."

"As do I," Tartran answered. "And the truth of the matter has yet to be seen. I come to you for answers, for murderous plots and attacks on my house and my line. I would have the truth of that before your revelry causes another war."

"And the accused" -- Ovorion turned bright green eyes to the kneeling noble --"will speak the truth."

"Your version of it?" Tartran asked. "Because there is *your* kind of truth, and there is real truth."

"The real truth." Ovorion nodded, never taking his eyes from Lord Claddafin. "In my presence, all those who accept me as their king must speak the real truth as you call it. Isn't that right, Lord Claddafin, also known as the Bold?"

"I -- it is so, Your Majesty," Lord Claddafin gasped, paling further as the words were all but torn from his throat.

Vulwin could feel the intricate spells take effect... it seemed as if a complicated loyalty spell had been invoked, probably when the lord took his oath of fealty to his king. It was unbreakable and undeniable. Vulwin wrapped his arms around his mate and sat back to watch the show.

"King Tartran Snoraxel, His Shining Majesty, has come forward today to bring charge against you, Claddafin." Ovorion spoke forcefully, so all in the hall could hear. "The king claims that twice you deliberately attempted to destroy his only son, and line. On the first attempt you tried to kill Vulwin, and on the second, you tried to transform him into one of those cursed to a half-life. Is this true?"

As the accusations issued forth from Ovorion's mouth, each one fell like lead, the weight of the Elvhen king's magical power infusing each one with a demand for the truth. Claddafin struggled for a moment before he dropped his head and began to speak. "I -- it... is... true."

The watching nobles grew eerily silent as they watched this drama unfold. The hall was so quiet the only sound that could be heard was Claddafin's ragged breathing.

"Explain." Ovorion snapped out the words, his eyes narrowing in anger as his wife gripped his arm in shock.

"I -- I... He murdered my son!" Claddafin finally bellowed as if holding back the words pained him, and knowing Elvhen magic, it probably had. "Vulwin the Silver murdered my son, and none of you bastards did anything about it!"

"Murdered." King Ovorion snorted, staring down at his subject. "You mean the same son who went to neutral territory in the Dhroven lands and murdered one of the king's line for an illegal Dragon stone? The same son who then stole valuables from his victim and attempted to hide out in the magical world? *That* son?"

The watching Elvhen paled, realizing what this could mean, and several who knew made their way silently moved toward the exits only to be stopped by a huge, hissing black familiar and several of the Dhroven king's elite guard.

"He just wanted to make his own way!" Claddafin roared. "The family business --"

"Of murdering Dragons, perhaps?" King Ovorion asked, ice forming along the walls of the hall as he spoke. "Of perhaps starting another Dragon war with the Dhrow as their allies?"

"He wasn't supposed to mate him!" Claddafin shouted. "The Dragon was supposed to break free and butcher him and his line. He was supposed to have been made half-dead then, but the bastard prince took the Dragon to mate. Who mates those monsters? They are only good as hounds you control or as spare parts on some mage's table. He was supposed to die! The king was supposed to die in protecting him! Everyone knows that the king's one weakness is his dual-eyed brat. They were supposed to pay!"

"Well," Vulwin drawled in the silence that fell as Claddafin glared at him and his mate. "That was a bit more intricate than what I worked out."

"You took the Dragon to mate. That is unheard of, and my family line specializes in Dragons. He should have turned you half-dead and killed the king for being party to his entrapment. That is what all the books have to say."

"And the books were wrong." Vulwin snickered while Iffear asked, "What books?"

Both were ignored.

"You told me you offered recompense for your son's wrongs and it was a murder attempt." King Ovorion nodded. "Clever wording, more clever than I gave you credit for. But do go on. How about this second plot to make him half-dead?"

"I made him half-dead." Claddafin grinned. "You can feel the coldness of death on him. My plan worked. The duel-eyed bastard is trapped, and the Dragon will go mad and turn against him."

"Really?" Vulwin drawled. "Because I feel quite fine, really, I do."

"I gave a Dragon stone to a Pixie." He ignored the gasps of anger at the words Dragon stone and tried to carry on as his fellow nobles started shouting questions.

"They were all destroyed for the peace pact! Where did you get one?" and "Did you murder someone to make one?" and the more popular, "How did you do that? That magic was lost!"

"I gave the Pixies a Dragon stone," he went on, talking over the shouted questions. "I gave them a stone that I poisoned. I dipped it in mercury salts." He grinned. "On my land, there is a cursed spring. We used to hide harvested Dragon remains there in the days of the founding of our line. Over time it became too poisonous to use and my ancestors discovered alternate ways of discarding unwanted Dragon parts, but the spring still exists. I soaked that cursed Dragon stone for days until the poisons took. Then I added my own to the stone."

"So you tried to kill the Dragon." King Ovorion shook his head at his noble "That was incredibly stupid."

"I don't want him dead. It wouldn't have killed him. It would have made him sick. The Pixies I gave it to wanted Dragon parts. They came to me. I gave them the lure. It was perfect. They were supposed to lure him out and then give it to him... or die when he took it. Either way, the Dragon would have reclaimed his precious stone."

"So you have now involved another race in your plot." King Ovorion shot a look to a nearby noble, and he immediately conjured a scroll, whispering into it before waving it out of existence, a message no doubt for Byrnexia Rilotus, the Pixies' queen.

"They came to me," Claddafin snapped. "They came to me and I didn't see a reason not to use them."

"And knowing that this would not kill the Dragon prince, you gave it to them anyway."

"I did not want his death. I wanted the bastard prince's suffering!" Claddafin raged as he fisted his hands in his hair. His wounds were rapidly healing, and he was moving easier, surrounded by the magic of his people, but it didn't seem to affect his sanity much.

"I wanted him to suffer the way I suffered, to know the death of a child. And he can only have one," Claddafin chortled, beyond defending himself. "You can only have one, Silver Prince. And now that one is lost to you! How does that make you feel? I hope it eats at your heart. I hope you wake screaming about it. I hope you can't eat because of it. I hope the thought of it makes your skin crawl and makes you vomit in regret. I hope it kills you by inches for all your pathetic half-life, for your eternity. I hope you recount it when everything you love dies and turns to dust, and you are left alone with nothing but the memory of what could have been! Even then, you won't feel one tenth of the agony that I go through. I hope it rots your soul. I hope it makes you scream when we all pass on to the next realm, and even when this land ends and it becomes the void, I hope you are still there screaming, remembering your loss."

The hatred in those words was obvious, and Claddafin smiled sweetly as he gloated about the success of his plans but...

"That would have been a downer," Vulwin agreed in the shocked silence, "except for a few things. One, my mate was never with child."

That bombshell pulled the smile right off Claddafin's face. His face fell blank. "Bullshit, as the humans say. That Dragon was in heat."

"Yes, but there is this wonderful thing called contraception. So while the whole of the realm knew that my mate was in heat when we bonded, after you attempted to use him as a murder weapon, there was no child created of our union because of contraception. So sorry."

Claddafin was motionless, but his eyes were huge blue pits of anger, an anger so deep it would not allow him to move or to speak, just to sit and listen.

"Next, in case you have not been paying attention, you just admitted to trying to murder the royal line. Yes, making me half-dead would mean that I could never take my father's throne and would in fact mean that you effectively killed my line... and that of the only royal line of the Dhrovish nation. You see, an attack against me is a direct attack against the throne. That means that your petty revenge against me is in fact an act of war. You attempted to disrupt and destroy a whole nation. You tried to murder all who are called Dhrow."

Claddafin was shaking his head, and Vulwin helpfully contradicted him. "Don't shake your head at me, Claddafin. You attempted to create a power vacuum in our kingdom, in our nation, a vacuum that would have destroyed you all." He offered him a grin as he nodded. "Yes, Claddafin. You forget that the Dragonish are now of my line and my mate would have taken the throne if I had been deemed unfit as a half-dead and unable to put issue on the throne. And the murder of a mate is a cue for the Dragon-warriors to fly again."

Claddafin paled as he cut his eyes to Iffear, who offered him a cheery wave, and then to the cold, dead eyes of his king. "Your Majesty --"

"I'm not done," Vulwin cut him off. "In your first and second attempts, you also tried to commit regicide of a sitting monarch, an offense so great that we can demand the destruction of your entire line, close-blooded or not. So you alone would not be punished for your crimes. You have doomed all that carry your tainted blood."

There were several nervous titters and angry hisses at that. It appeared that Lord Claddafin was related to a lot of nobles and had placed their existence on a hard, dark gamble -- and lost.

"Am I missing anything, Father?" Vulwin asked as he looked to where his father stood.

"Only that attempting to murder me is pointless as you have not yet reached your full maturity. I am beautifully unkillable."

Claddafin's face exploded in a color so red it was nearly purple as he began to choke on his own anger.

"And now I have a question." King Tartran stepped forward, his right hand and lover at his side. Kno looked angered beyond belief, the whole, placid calm air he usually projected stripping away with every step, to show the anger and rage of someone who was half-dead.

A lust for vengeance stood clearly on the king's face. The knowledge that he instead would have probably faced the fate that Claddafin predicted for the prince was made painfully aware to him. The fact that he could tip over into insanity from the attempted loss of his child made him the scariest being in the room now, save for the Dragon in human guise who had smoke trickling from his nose. "Where are the rest of the Dragon Stones, the grimoire used to create them, and the implements of murder that your line did not turn over as the peace pact required? You, Lord Claddafin, are not only treasonous to your own people; you just laid the instruments for all Elvhen destruction at my feet."

Claddafin whimpered and looked to his king, who had risen to his feet, his expression black before he turned away, a public and very direct cut.

"Your Majesty..." Claddafin's words trailed off as he looked around at his fellow nobles... all of whom, one by one, turned their backs on him. He was alone. The future that he had planned for Vulwin was now his present.

"I want those stones, the means to create more, and any implement or creation of the Dragonish people. I also demand any forbidden information about them, and I want them before me now." By the time King Tartran was done speaking, he was shouting the words, angered beyond belief. "Are my words not heard? I want them now, or I'll start picking off nobles to your line... starting with the queen."

There was a gasp at his words, and even the Elvhen king had no say in this. He cast pained eyes to his lovely wife, helplessness apparent. It was her or the whole of the Elvhen nation, and a ruler had to protect his people.

"I had no idea he was doing this," the queen finally spoke. "But yes, my line is loosely related to Claddafin's and generations gone by. We are connected, which allows him the use of my Lord Husband's moniker, The Bold. I should have known when he presented me with this necklace" -- she ran her fingers over bejeweled chains --"that something was off about it. I can see it almost matches the design that Prince Iffear now wears. This is of Dragonish make, is it not?" She turned to her cousin. "You stole it and mutilated it and presented it to me as a gift and a reminder of our shared heritage, Claddafin. Did it make you smile to see a relic from the people your line, our line, attempted to destroy, sitting on the throne? Did it make you feel closer to royalty?"

She reached up and unclasped the necklace, the heavy chains falling into her hands. She strode off of the dais that held the matching royal thrones and boldly walked over to Iffear, holding the chains between both hands carefully.

"Prince Iffear, I believe this belongs to you." The nobles were now turning back around, staring at the queen as she humbled herself to a foreign prince. Queen Alyae Torrae spoke honestly and plainly as she observed Iffear.

"It is not of my direct line, but I recognize the remains of the magic in it. It is from a line of artisans, the first line to fall to the Elvhen madness we called The Hunt. It was the destruction of this very line that sparked off the beginnings of the Dragon Wars that devastated both of our peoples," replied Iffear.

"Praise the Fates I can return it," Alyae gasped, pressing the necklace into his hands. "This should have never been in our possession."

"I am waiting," King Tartran interrupted as he nodded for Kno to go to the queen's side. The sound of him unseating his red-bladed sword dripping in madness and death, brought a whimper to the Elvhen king's throat and real fear in his eyes before he could cover it up under a concerned mask. Apparently, King Ovorion loved his queen. This was tearing him up inside, to be so helpless in the face of something so minor that could begin the extermination of all his people.

Claddafin remained stubbornly silent.

Shrugging, Kno fisted his blade in his hands before addressing the queen. "My word, Your Majesty Queen Alyae Torrae the Brave, it will be quick and painless. I honor your life as much as I honor your death."

With crystalline tears running down her face, the Elvhen queen nodded and lowered her head, parting her hair to make it easier for his blade to find her bare neck.

Kno lifted his blade in both hands, red dripping

down to cover the hilt and coat his hands, hissing and smoking, then --

"Stop!" There was a flash, and the Pixie queen popped into existence. "Please wait!"

The tiny queen appeared in a flash of swirling pink magic, and with her came a small army of Pixie Fae, decked out formally, and not for war. But what was most interesting was the young Fae who came with her.

"Father," the tall, pale Elvhen female, snarled as she stalked forward. "What did you do?"

"Why, your father committed treason and is in the midst of starting a war." King Tartran motioned to Kno to step back. The half-dead warrior retired a step, re-sheathing his sword and shaking his hands free of the red fluid that coated the blade, revealing his hands in perfect condition though the ground hissed where the droplets of red had fallen.

"Does that not... burn?" Queen Alyae asked, raising her head and unashamedly not wiping her tears away. "That looks painful."

"The pain reminds me that I am alive." Kno offered a bow as he turned toward his king.

"I received your message," the Pixie queen, Byrnexia Rilotus, addressed King Ovorion as he sat paralyzed on his throne, watching the slaughter of his wife being postponed. "I read what you had written, what three of mine had been doing in the human realm, and I adhered to your request as a minor atonement. I have brought this one's remaining daughter before you as requested. She is the eldest and far more mature than her brothers, who are also in hiding at their father's request. She knows nothing of what has transpired here today, and I hope her presence can temper things and return a little balance."

"So you bring me someone of his direct line to kill," Vulwin's father mused. "This is lovely, yet I still prefer the queen. Makes a solid statement, does it not?" He nudged Claddafin with his boot. "Or maybe killing her will make you acquiesce, and return what your line has stolen and abused for generations."

"Father!" the dark-haired Fae screamed. "You would see the murder of our queen?"

When he didn't respond, she turned to King Tartran. "Please, sire, tell me what you desire from us, and I will deliver it. Anything to prevent this. Anything!"

"I require the Dragon Stones that your father hoards. I want all the items of Dragonish make and design that he and your ancestors have stolen over the years, and I want them all now."

"Your will be done." She nodded, and Claddafin roared out in anger and denial.

"No!" his daughter shouted back, striking her father across the face and knocking him back on his ass. "You court war? Is this your vengeance? Innocents suffering and dying while you sit there trying to justify each death because of your stupidity, ignoring the fact that it was our line who started this?"

"You -- you knew about this?" The Elvhen king's voice was rough as he finally addressed Claddafin's daughter. "You knew?"

"I knew what our family once was." She dropped to her knees before her king. "I knew what we were, but I had no idea that we were still... active. Father all but worships our line's progenitors, and neither I nor most of my brothers and sisters could understand why. No, Your Majesty. I had no idea what my father has been doing, but I have a good idea where he has been keeping his hoard."

"Go on," the Elvhen king prompted.

"There is a cavern on the southernmost tip of our lands. It is where the ancestral manor once stood. Father and some of my brothers and cousins would often make pilgrimages there. Those of us who did not honor the line as he felt we should were excluded. I am sure that is where he keeps his stash of dangerous and stolen goods."

"And is there a hot spring there?" Iffear asked, and the young lady started as he stepped forward, nodding slowly.

"It is forbidden as it is poisoned by some naturally occurring stone."

"Cinnabar," Iffear grumbled, explaining to King Ovorion and Vulwin. "It is well known that parts of our physiology, our bones and our manes, transform into cinnabar once our life has expired. And if they have been tossing our bones and remains into a hot spring --"

"Then the whole damn land is tainted, cursed." Tartran shared a look with his son. "No wonder the whole fucking line is mad."

"And this taint will eventually spread throughout my lands, yes, Prince Iffear?" the Elvhen king asked.

"There is a reason one is consider cursed when they murder a Dragon," Iffear answered. "It is not just the Dragon-rage and that Dragon-flame that one must be wary of."

"Take the land," the young noblewoman called out as the queen walked over to her and pulled her to her feet. "Take it all. Please... just... I don't want our family to be the cause of our extinction. I don't want it to be war. Please."

"Will this sate your anger, King Tartran

Snoraxel?" the Elvhen king asked. "Will this quench your desire for Elvhen blood?"

"It is a start." Tartran nodded, and Kno at once returned to his side. "But I want all the stones and I want them now."

"It will be done," the noblewoman promised. "Just please... please... no more deaths, King Tartran. Please. I beseech you."

"Your pleas are heard and do not move me." Vulwin's father finally spoke directly to her. "But I have no wish to engage in a war of attrition, for this is what it would be. Our people are quite matched in combat style and resources," he acknowledged "but we have the Dragons on our side. A war between us would be determined by who has the greater resources. Although I am positive the Dhrovish people would rise triumphant, I don't believe either of our sides can endure such losses. A war between us would turn this very realm into a dark void, much like what remains of the battlefield of the Gray Gulf."

"So how will your thirst for vengeance be quenched?" King Ovorion asked as his wife stepped up to the dais and once again reclaimed her spot at his side.

"The way I see things," Tartran mused, "is that we have both been wronged. I want this fool and all those who followed him dead. No negotiations. I want those Dragon Stones and those stolen Dragon artifacts and all the knowledge that pertains to his dark arts delivered posthaste. I would consider that a start. The rest of our grievances can be aired and decided in private."

"Sounds a fair solution and far better than war," Ovorion agreed.

"Or the death of your mate." King Tartran

offered him a smile. "No offense, Queen Alyae Torrae, so named by my second as The Brave."

"None taken." She offered him a gracious smile. Although tight, it was obvious she was relieved to be back in the presence and the safety of her king. "And I gladly accept the name bequeathed to me by your second. Yet I believe the brave one here is my husband. He stood fast and brave and would have allowed the death of one he loves to save his people."

Claddafin remained silent, broken, and stayed that way as his daughter called for servants to break into the remains of the manor and bring forth all that was called for.

In the end, there were over twelve grimoires filled with forbidden magic and enchantments to lure, capture, and ultimately kill Dragons. There were very graphic and detailed drawings that made Vulwin feel sick just looking at them. There were uncounted Dragon artifacts, tools, and jewelry in trunks that seemed to keep being delivered, and the most horrifying discovery of them all -- close to three hundred active Dragon Stones. Then the huge lead-lined oak and rowan trunk that held them was opened, and both Iffear and Vulwin were brought to their knees by the explosion of fear and pain.

"By the Fates," King Tartran gasped, and even the Elvhen king, who was not connected to the stones in any way, clutched at his chest in pain when the trunk was opened.

"Close it!" Vulwin demanded as Iffear began to quiver in his arms. "Close it now! It's too much!"

When the trunk slammed shut, unashamed, Iffear dissolved into silent tears, his whole body shaking with the memory of the screams and cries of three hundred trapped souls.

"They need to be sung to rest," Vulwin explained as Kno and his father and their guard surrounded the Dragon prince. "They... they are suffering, Father." Vulwin wiped away his own tears. "They are in agony."

"Then it will be done." Tartran rested his hand on his son's shoulder as they all mourned for the lives stolen and trapped to be used for this madness. "When you compose yourself, leave this place. Do what must be done. We" -- he motioned to Kno and his remaining guards -- "will ensure that this peace will last. You have done enough, my son. Get you and your mate to safety. We will handle the rest."

Chapter Five

They decided on the Gray Gulf. It was an easy decision to make as this site was close to the first stone they'd laid together. It was a place where the many souls would find peace amidst the silence of the many deaths that had drained the place of all life.

They didn't wait as they had to on the human world because this realm, their true realm, was made of magic.

"A political choice?" Iffear asked as he observed the fields packed with Dhrow who had come to pay homage and honor those who never had a chance at existence. What surprised him was the large number of Elvhen who'd invited themselves and willingly stood amidst the Dhrow to show their regret that one of their own had perpetrated such a despicable act, no matter how many years ago the stones had been made, and to show a willingness to dwell in peace with their fellow Fae.

"No," Vulwin whispered to his lover who stood at his side, dressed in his bejeweled finery. "It just felt right."

Neither his father nor the Elvhen king were there; they were still working out what it would take to repair the small peace that they had found. It was understood, though, that his father, at least, wished to be there with them on this solemn occasion. In his place he had sent several of his advisers and half of his personal guard. Not only was this a show of trust, it went to prove to all just how dangerous the Shining King on the Dhrovish throne actually was. Unkillable still and not afraid to exploit it.

This time Vulwin did not have to create a magical circle. Every bit of land in the Fae realm was magic. The hateful trunk was opened once more, and the amber-colored stones carefully laid out in a widening round of circles. It was a beautiful, glittering circle that spoke of more pain and anguish than many had ever perceived. It was an unspeakable perversion of magic and against all that the Fae claimed sacred. It was such a terrible pervasive thing that even those not magically gifted felt the pinch of it, and the Pixies, who came out in full force, were nearly staggered by the weight of the terrible grief the stones held. Then it was time. It was only for him and his Dragon to call the ceremony to order, to open their hearts and their magic... and sing.

The song that they sang had no words. It was a beautiful melding of tunes. As if compelled by magic, Vulwin and Iffear opened their mouths, let their heads fall back, and they sang. From their hearts, they sang. From the bottom of their souls, they sang. From their cores poured forth a sweet cacophony that brought the watching Fae to their knees. From the land, the ashy gray land that still held on to the deaths of a thousand years ago, sprang forth a new magic. It flowed from the once dead ground and into their bodies, causing Vulwin's hair to fly around him, his silver sparkles to glisten like stars in the midnight sky that turned his bass voice into nothing more than an instrument of the Fates. Iffear's eyes glistened, his scale pattern formed all over his body as the vibrant colors of green and black swirled along his skin. The jewels that bespeckled his chains shrouding his body began to glisten and glow, enhancing his powerful tenor voice until the ground beneath their feet began to shake and the air around them began to vibrate with their power.

They sang, eyes closed, hands extended, until tears rained down from their eyes, until their bodies began to quake and their muscles gave way. Collapsing onto the gray earth, they sang until it felt like their very souls were being ripped from their bodies to give strength to the powerful song that poured forth.

The watching Fae began to hum uncontrollably, the magic from their own cores being pulled from them by magic. They added a harmony that was fit for the gods. Their voices began to rise in counterpoint to the song that Vulwin and Iffear were singing. And then... one by one the amber stones began to rise.

As if lifted by an unseen hand, the stones flowed up from the ground and began to quiver. They spun and danced in a sudden wind that blew them upward toward the heavens. They spun and they shook until the first one shattered. With the sound of tinkling crystal, the amber stone shattered and the sliver of a soul inside burst free. That first was followed by another and still another until the sound of shattering stones nearly drowned out the songs of the singers.

Then their colors began to flow. Reds and green, black and blues, browns and yellows and pinks... All the colors of the spectrum burst forth and with them the sound of childish laughter. Crying out their freedom, the slivers of souls burst forth and began playfully winding around the singers, playing in hair pulled free by the wind, kissing their cheeks, caressing their faces. The colors swirled and danced and laughed until almost as if an invisible signal had been given, they rose up toward the heavens. Faster and faster they fled until a cyclone of vibrant colors swirled about the land. Finally, in one electric burst, they shot up into the sky, a silver-white flash... And then they were no more. The song had come to an end... yet the magic there remained.

It started as a bright flash of green beneath the ground where Iffear and Vulwin lay, just a small speck of green in the midst of all that drab gray. Then it began to spread. The speck grew wider and wider until it began to pour out in waves, flooding over the land. A wave of green so great and so thick it lifted the Fae from their feet. Then it exploded, a flowing of lush greenery that shot over the land, climbed up dead trees, flowing over the remains of death with new life.

The Fae watched in awe, chattering and laughing their joy -- Dhrow, Pixie, Elvhen; it made no difference. The magic in them all rejoiced... because what were the Fae other than the conduit for magic to work her great mysteries?

And for Vulwin and Iffear, they saw and felt nothing, sleeping and recovering in the gentle embrace of magic themselves. They lay, avatars of this great work, recovering and basking in the sweet release of death and in the warm embrace of new life.

* * *

Days passed and the pair slept, carried home by King Tartran's guard. They rested in the Silver Prince's chambers, wrapped around each other in a way that prevented any and all from separating them. A servant was charged with looking over them, and when she went tearing down the hall to the king's personal chambers, Tartran and Kno were more than ready to welcome the two princes back to the land of the living.

Vulwin was the first to open his eyes. He recognized the ceiling. He was flat on his back, wrapped around his mate, and... The ceiling. He was in his father's palace.

He turned his head to see Iffear snoring lightly beside him, his face relaxed and his body loose in his repose. "Beautiful," he whispered, and the sound of his own voice, scratchy and rough, shocked him into full awareness.

"Rest easy, my son." Tartran was standing at his bedside, and that was almost enough to make Vulwin jump to attention, yet his body was too weak to respond. "You are safe."

"What happened?" he asked finally, relaxing back into the plush blankets that surrounded them.

"Your core. You drained it and nearly shattered it singing the Dragon Stones to rest."

"I barely remember that," Vulwin spoke softly, wrinkling his nose at the sound of his voice.

"It was weeks ago."

"Weeks --"

"Weeks. King Ovorion and I are still in discussions but for now, the peace holds."

"Lord Claddafin, what of him?"

"Do you know that magical familiars of Dragons take something of their masters with them?" Tartran almost looked disturbed as he took a seat beside his son.

"Well, it is to be expected. Iffear has a tight bond with his familiar, an unusually strong bond."

"And his ability to spit Dragon fire." Tartran shuddered as be began to relay the tale. "Chinsie burned... all the affected sons alive on a pyre of the forbidden tomes of magic they hoarded. The Pixies, in atonement for what their clansmen had done, also searched the properties and found many more implements of torture, more magical grimoires and scrolls, and preserved Dragon parts. They were all placed on the fire, and I believe Chinsie relished their screams of pain as the short-ears burned."

Vulwin thought of the tame black cat, of how she transformed into a monster to protect her master.

"Yeah, I can see that. She is an intimidating little creature."

"Dragon-flame will burn until it is recalled," Tartran continued. "She pulled the flames back to herself and swallowed them. It was a most... impressive sight."

"You mean she scared the hell out of you and all who watched."

"To be blunt, yes." Tartran gave a delicate shudder. "I am given to understand that her protection extends to you as well, Vulwin. I am pleased to have you so well-guarded."

"Really?" Vulwin snorted, recalling all the times when he'd needed his father, and the king was too busy to be bothered.

"Really." The king wrinkled his nose, looking exactly like his son for a moment. "This hostility you have toward me is unseemly."

"Really?" Vulwin drawled back before he just gasped, "Fuck it. You want to know why I'm hostile to you after all you did?" He all but sneered the word. "You don't understand --"

"I tried my best, Vulwin."

"You sent me away."

"I had to." His father tried to explain, but Vulwin was not having it.

"When other younglings were racing home to tell their fathers of their advances, I got to run home to a cold room and maybe Kno praising what I had accomplished. When other boys were hurt and running to their fathers for comfort, you were the only one I know of to tell his son that he would recover, so stop whining, that nothing could kill him at that stage of life."

"It was the truth."

"Instead of tales of your adventures, I was taught protocol and strategy."

"Necessary for your development."

"Bullshit," Vulwin snapped. "My father was necessary for my development and he was never there. You want to explain that one, Father? I thought the Dhrow were supposed to love their sons above all else, so I spent decades thinking that something must be wrong with me, that I must be defective in some way to not earn the slightest bit of tenderness from my own father."

"I was scared," Tartran finally shouted, losing his kingly poise. "I was scared, Vulwin. I didn't know what to do. I loved your mother, loved her more than myself. I loved her so hard and so fast that most thought it was an illness in me. I loved her beyond all reason, and I did what I could to not make her pregnant. We went for centuries, just the two of us, living and loving... I thought I had it all. I thought I was truly blessed. And then... then she stopped taking her contraception. She threw herself into my lap one day and told me she was pregnant. I thought my world had come to an end, Vulwin, because that meant her death. My silver-eyed lass was going to leave me. And do you know why she did that? Do you?"

"No," Vulwin spoke softly, eyes wide at seeing so much emotion from a father that had previously posed as a cold slab of stone.

"Because humans are not meant to be long-lived. She said as happy as she was, she had grown tired of her existence. I never lied to her; she knew what she was getting herself into by mating with me, by agreeing to be mine, and yet her spirit -- it began to fade. Humans were not meant to live forever, she told me. She loved me but she was ready to pass on to the next realm... and the only gift she could think to give to me was a son to love. And I loved you, Vulwin. You... You look so much like her. She had freckles. They were dusted all over her body like someone had sprinkled her with sunshine -- your freckles. And her eyes... they were as silver as your left one. You looked so much like her and you had her spirit, my son. Beholding you was just like having a piece of her. And then I became afraid. Her death almost ended me, Vulwin. I didn't want to live until I saw you. All that fear transferred to you. I had to leave your upbringing to others because I would have chained you to my side. You would have never become a warrior, you would have been weak and smothered by my love. And then you grew capable and strong. I knew I had to send you away or I would have chained you to me as an advisor. You never would have become the Dhrow who you are today if I had interfered. Everything you have you earned by your own two hands and you were safe from the dangerous stupidity that so often is couched as games and played here. And then... the Dragon. I took one look at him and knew that if you were paired, you would never have to deal with the heartbreak that nearly brought me low. A Dragon is magic, Vulwin. And where Dhrow always breed true, Dragons can conceive by any creature of magic."

"They are wild magic," Vulwin agreed.

"Yes, they are creatures of magic. And the magic would not take him away from you. You would have your son... and if he wanted more he would be able to bear Dragons, Vulwin. You may only have one son, but a Dragon can bear as many offspring as they want. You would never have to deal with the pain of loving a mate who would leave you and you could have many children at your feet, issue for the throne and children of the heart." He smiled. "And the contraception on the ring... that was so that you could learn to love your mate, love him as I loved your mother. I -- I just want so much for you, Vulwin. I don't want you to be burned with pain."

Vulwin was silent, absorbing what his father told him. "I -- I didn't know."

"And I should have told you. Kno warned me eons ago that in my caution to see you safe from all that harmed you, I would drive you away... and it appeared I succeeded."

"Father --"

"Vulwin. Just know that I love you, my son. I have always loved you and I will never stop loving you. You are my heart and soul, the very core of me." He shook his head softly. "You look so much like her and yet I can only see the mature male that you have become. I am so very proud of you."

The king rose to his feet and moved toward the door when Iffear poked Vulwin in the side sharply. "If you love him, tell him. Don't make the same mistakes," his mate warned, his slitted eyes red and glowing.

"You were awake --"

"Tell him!"

"I love you too," Vulwin called out, the words seemingly ripped from his sore throat. "Father... I... I love you too."

King Tartran paused for a moment, his body seeming to go weak for a moment, before he recovered himself and turned to smile at his son.

"This I know." His flitting black eyes looked like they were filled with tears.

"You know nothing, Shining Majesty," Vulwin groused. "And you fool no one."

His father's sniff and Kno's knowing voice

chiming out, "Told you so," was the last things he heard before his door was closed.

"You were awake?"

"Who could sleep with all that talk of emotions going on?" Iffear asked, snuggling down to nuzzle him. "Seriously, are you okay?"

"I -- I spent my whole life trying to make that Fae love me, approve of me... and I had his love all along."

"Stubborn folk, these, Dhrow," Iffear teased.

"Stubborn, but with a marvelous capacity to learn. And in knowing that, Iffear, I have to say..." He sighed deeply, freeing a hand to caress his mate's face. "I... I examined our bond... and my feelings have... I need to tell you --"

"I love you too, my Dhrow." Iffear chuckled.

"How did... I mean -- did you see the blue --"

"No. I have not put our bond to any kind of examination, Vulwin. I just followed my heart. I knew. I love you, my mate. And I am pleased that you love me as well, though you had to examine our bond to discover the truth of your own emotions."

"It's a failing," Vulwin agreed. "I got it from my father."

That got him a laughing kiss as they snuggled together in his childhood bed.

"I can't wait to go back home," Vulwin finally whispered as they both began to fall asleep. "Home with a Brownie and a familiar and Starbucks and designer jeans... you know, all the things that make our abode a home."

"Really?" Iffear pressed a sleepy kiss to the mating mark on his neck. "To me, home is wherever you are."

And after he spoke those words so sweetly, it was several hours before they could rest. After all, a

Dhrow, even a stubborn one, had to show his mate how much he loved him... even if that meant hours of screaming sex and several very draining orgasms.

Stephanie Burke

Have You Been Flashed?

Stephanie is a *USA Today Best Selling* multi-published, multi-award-winning author, Master Costumer, handicapped, wife and mother of two.

From sex shifting shape-shifting Dragons to undersea worlds, up to sexually confused elemental fey and homoerotic mysteries, all the way to pastel challenged urban sprites, Stephanie has done it all, and hopes to do more.

Stephanie is an orator on her favorite subject of writing and world building, a sometimes teacher when you feed her enough tea and donuts, an anime nut, a costumer, and a frequent guest of various sci-fi and writing cons where she can be found leading panel discussions or researching more and varied legends and theories to improve her writing skills.

Stephanie is known for her love of the outrageous, strong female characters, believable worlds, male characters filled with depth, and multi-cultural stories that make the reader sit up and take notice.

Stephanie at Changeling: changelingpress.com/stephanie-burke-a-30

Changeling Press E-Books

More Sci-Fi, Fantasy, Paranormal, and BDSM adventures available in e-book format for immediate download at ChangelingPress.com -- Werewolves, Vampires, Dragons, Shapeshifters and more -- Erotic Tales from the edge of your imagination.

What are E-Books?

E-books, or electronic books, are books designed to be read in digital format -- on your desktop or laptop computer, notebook, tablet, Smart Phone, or any electronic e-book reader.

Where can I get Changeling Press E-Books?

Changeling Press e-books are available at ChangelingPress.com, Amazon, Apple Books, Barnes & Noble, and Kobo/Walmart.

Changeling Press, LLC

ChangelingPress.com